PRAIRIE SCHOONER BOOK PRIZE IN FICTION

EDITOR   *Kwame Dawes*

ONE-
HUNDRED-
KNUCKLED
FIST

STORIES

Dustin M. Hoffman

UNIVERSITY OF NEBRASKA PRESS   *Lincoln and London*

Acknowledgments for the use
of copyrighted material appear
on page ix, which constitutes an
extension of the copyright page.

Library of Congress Cataloging-
in-Publication Data
Names: Hoffman, Dustin M., author.
Title: One-hundred-knuckled fist:
stories / Dustin M. Hoffman.
Description: Lincoln: University of
Nebraska Press, 2016. | Series: Prairie
Schooner book prize in fiction
Identifiers: LCCN 2015047729
ISBN 9780803288546 (pbk.: alk. paper)
ISBN 9780803288966 (epub)
ISBN 9780803288973 (mobi)
ISBN 9780803288980 (pdf)
Subjects: LCSH: Blue collar
workers—Fiction. | Working class—
Fiction. | Middle West—Fiction.
Classification: LCC PS3608.O477666
A6 2016 | DDC 813/.6—dc23 LC record
available at http://lccn.loc.gov/2015047729

Set in Chaparral by Rachel Gould.
Designed by N. Putens.

For Carrie

All people who work with their hands are partly invisible, and the more important the work they do, the less visible they are.

—GEORGE ORWELL

CONTENTS

ACKNOWLEDGMENTS

THANKS TO ALL THE MAGAZINES AND THEIR EDITORS WHO first supported and shaped the stories in this collection:

Black Warrior Review for first publishing "Pushing the Knives"

Juked for "One-Hundred-Knuckled Fist"

Sou'wester for "Sawdust and Glue"

Phoebe for "Can Picking"

Quarter after Eight for "Everything a Snake Needs"

Blue Mesa Review for "The Fire Chasers"

Witness for "Subdivision Accidents"

MAKE for "Ice-Cream Dream"

Cimarron Review for "Conch Tongue"

Yemassee for "One More for You"

Copper Nickel for "Strong as Paper Men"

Midwestern Gothic for reprinting "Strong as Paper Men"

Puerto del Sol for "Building Walls"

Fourteen Hills for "Workmen's Compensation"

Threepenny Review for "Touching in Texas"

Thanks to the editors and wonderful folks at *Prairie Schooner* and University of Nebraska Press: Kwame Dawes, Ashley Strosnider,

Elizabeth Nunez, Bernardine Evaristo, Courtney Ochsner, Marguerite Boyles, Joeth Zucco, and Jeremy Hall. Your faith in this book and the hard work you put into it mean the world to me.

Thanks to my professors at Bowling Green State University and Western Michigan University who helped me find my voice, especially Wendell Mayo, Lawrence Coates, Michael Czyzniejewski, Theresa Williams, Jaimy Gordon, Thisbe Nissen, Jon Adams, and Nancy Eimers. Thanks to my first writing teacher and great friend, Adam Schuitema.

Thanks to my inspiring, talented friends who made my years at BGSU so precious, especially Aimee Pogson, Megan Ayers, Stephanie Marker, Anne Valente, Jacqueline Vogtman, Brad Modlin, and Matt Bell. Thanks also to my brilliant friends from WMU, especially Dan Mancilla, Jeffrey Otte, Katie Burpo, Elissa Cahn, Laurie Cedilnik, David Johnson, Annie Strother, and Bridget Dooley. Thanks to Brandon Davis Jennings for reading everything I've ever written and for always making me do it better. And thanks to Joseph Celizic, my magic editor, for always believing in my work stories.

Thanks to the tradesmen and tradeswomen who told me stories while we painted or roofed or sanded drywall, especially Jason Griffin, Jeremy Brown, Quincy, Tom, Craig and Margot, all the Pats, Rob, Brent, Chandler Anderson, Celia, Doug, and Matthew Jeffrey. And thanks to my colleagues who showed me a different kind of work, especially Glenn Deutsch, Jacqui Nathan, Donna Nelson-Beene, Steve Feffer, Kim Ballard, and the amazing folks from the English departments at Albion College and Winthrop University.

Thanks to my family of strong women—my mom, Linda, and my sisters, Heather and Holly—and to my dad, Michael, who first trusted me to swing a paintbrush and run a saw. Thanks to the Binger family. Thanks to my brother-in-music Daniel McDonald. Thanks to my inspirations, my reasons to keep working hard, Evelyn Josephine and Alison Jane. Finally, thanks to my best friend, my love, the hardest worker I've ever known, Carrie.

ONE-HUNDRED-KNUCKLED FIST

PUSHING THE KNIVES

HE'S SUPPOSED TO BE PUSHING THE KNIVES. THRUSTING THEM up to the humming tube lighting of the supermarket so the polished steel sparkles, so you can almost hear the reflected twinkle slide across the blade. But gazing into vast ceilings, pure white girders grazed by boxed and shrink-wrapped bulk products towering in twenty-foot-tall aisles, makes him dizzy. He'd prefer to keep his head down. He should be showing off the sexy curves of the fillet knife, flaunting the no-nonsense power of the bulking cleaver. Instead, he runs his fingers over the name tag pinned to his white chef's uniform complete with the white hat that poofs at the top like an atomic mushroom cloud, his thinning hairline tightly concealed underneath the explosion. His name tag is bright gold. The grooves of his name are sharp and cut skillfully, deeply. It reads, "Wyatt." But how can he live up to "Wyatt" engraved in gold, sparkling in tube lights like the knives should be?

A woman with short brown hair barely stretched into a ponytail and wearing gray sweatpants pushes a cart toward his stand. One of the wheels squeaks shrilly. It reminds Wyatt of the tenor in his trainer's voice, the guy with the sharp triangle of black facial hair below his lower lip who wore the managerial navy-blue chef's uniform. His two weeks of training just ended yesterday, but he can still hear his trainer shrieking, *This is your target audience! Midthirties, slightly overweight, listless eyes that wander over shrink-wrapped ground chuck looking like red brains. Reel her in, Wyatt. Make the sale!* But he can't bring himself to do it. He is a pathetic salesman. Shy, terrible at talking. He feels lost in a forest of aisles the height of redwoods. He's glad to be standing near the meat, near squat, refrigerated troughs less daunting. Still, in front of him, colorful displays and bar codes stack to the ceiling, obscuring his vision, and he wonders if there are actually more people somewhere in this store. Is this lady in her sweatpants his lone audience member, his only shot? If he had any courage, he might scale an aisle, perch atop stacked two-hundred-unit diaper boxes, and proclaim his sales pitch.

The woman is close now. Almost to the steaks, near where his promotional stand sits, painted blue with a big yellow lightning bolt and a sign that reads THUNDER BLADES: STRIKE CULINARY PERFECTION. He wishes he had the wit and intensity his sign promises. She inches toward him, squeaking closer. This is his big moment, his first potential sale. He thinks back to his training manual, how he should approach this customer.

Ma'am, a moment of your precious time?

(Don't wait for her. Take it!)

Has your cutlery gone dull, uninspired, pointlessly pathetic? This is a common tragedy that befalls nearly nine of every ten households in America. A fact!

(Keep it up. Don't relent now. You've got the facts down; now show her the blades.)

Ha! Your troubles are solved!

(Brandish the Electroshocker Chef's Knife. But don't brandish too much; you don't want her to think you're a serial killer.)

On this planet, you won't find a sharper, more balanced knife. As if forged in the fires of Olympus, it slices with incomparable power and accuracy. But I could talk all day. The proof is in the results. Observe as the Electroshocker slices with perfection. There! Impossible? No. Amazing! And so easy a child could do it.

(Note: Don't sell knives to children under the age of ten. These things are sharp!)

A finer edge and I'd be splitting atoms. But there's more. So much more . . .

(Attaboy! That's how we do it!)

But he can't begin the pitch, can't dredge the words from his quivering abdomen. Standing so close to the steak troughs is freezing him. The frigid temperatures that keep grade-A meat fresh stop him cold. This seems like a valid excuse. He must remember to not be so hard on himself, but he always is.

And now she's front and center, her eyes looking him up and down. Him, not the knives, up and down. He straightens his posture, pushes out his flat pectorals, tries to smile with his yellowed teeth. It makes him worry. In training, they explained how important appearances are, how you're not just selling products, but yourselves. He remembers how desperately he needs tooth whiteners and Chuck Norris's abs machine. She looks away. He can't blame her. Her cart squeaks on toward the ice cream and frozen key lime pies. She is gone. No sale. No commission. No money for whiter teeth and abs of steel. It's okay; he'll get the next one. He's still learning.

"Why didn't you get *that* one?" His supervisor, Lee, bursts from his hiding spot at the endcap of the cereal aisle, scattering cardboard toucans across the tile floor. He is a good hider. Wyatt didn't even know he was there. It's an impressive skill. Lee is a fat man, but short. He must have rolled up like a hedgehog to stow himself in the bottom shelf behind all those cereal boxes.

"You didn't say a damn word." Lee is breathing hard. Droplets of sweat form on his round, bald, baby-faced head. Wyatt doesn't mean or want to disappoint him. He wants Lee to like him. But Lee will never be his friend until he starts making sales.

"Are you at least sawing the sledgehammer?"

Wyatt completely forgot about the sledgehammer. He fidgets with his name tag.

"Well, damn it." Lee pushes Wyatt out from the knife stand. He reaches under for the sledgehammer and thunks it down on the stand's massive oak cutting board. "You should be. You should have worked up a nice pile of shavings at this point. Start sawing for Christ's sake."

Wyatt unsheathes the serrated knife, the Thundertooth. Why didn't he remember the sledgehammer? It's sure to draw in customers. How could he be so absentminded? He draws the blade across the head of the sledge a few times, a few more. Metal sledge shavings sprinkle the cutting board, his fingers, his hands.

"That's the ticket! Show them what the knives can do. How they'll never go dull, even when it's steel against steel."

Lee squeezes himself back into the bottom shelf of the endcap. He indeed does look like a balled-up hedgehog, tucked knees clutched in his hairy arms. His face is less red now, but he still looks nervous. Lee has two teenage girls and a baby boy on the way. His kids' welfare depends on the sheer selling prowess of his regional salesmen. So much depends on Wyatt's sales pitch. Lee's daughters will not wear designer clothes and hence will never find lovers. The baby will not utter genius giggles at educational mobiles and will grow up dull-eyed, uninspired, and stupid. Wyatt hates the pressure piling up like the metal shavings. A light-gray line forms across the sledge head, where metal meets metal. A layer of shavings covers the stand top.

"Good. Great. Go get 'em, Wyatt. We're all behind you, rooting for you," Lee says, balled up in his hiding spot. "Now, before you get too far, cover me up with the cereal boxes again."

Wyatt picks the toucans off the floor and stacks them around Lee in a colorful, tropical igloo. He leaves a slot for Lee to peep through, even though he doesn't want to. He'd rather not have Lee watching him so closely. His presence is pressure, a reminder of all the lives at stake. He focuses on sawing.

He wonders if he's really cut out for this vocation. Before Thunder Blades, he worked in a nursing home called The Best Is Yet to Come. The residents thrived off his listening skills, stringing their stories along for hours. So many stories. But too many of the residents died in a freak outbreak of heart attacks and strokes and aneurysms. Everyone's circulatory system just went wonky one week, twenty-three all on one Wednesday. Clogged up or burst, and the nursing home staff needed to be cut in half. These things happen. Hearts explode or just stop. There was no one to blame, Wyatt tried to convince himself. But there must have been more he could have done, more stories he could have listened to, kept record of in his mind like a Venus flytrap of dead men's tales, which might have lessened the loads on their strained hearts.

One resident in particular, Mr. Henderson, never told him a story deep enough. He didn't want to share his family tree with Wyatt or to talk about children or even to reveal his first name. Instead, he told Wyatt about cars: his bright-yellow Bel Air with the sexy tail fins; the Crown Vic lined with red velvet upholstery, so sleek no ass deserved such classy cushioning. He told him about slinking California blacktop, windows down at sunset next to the ocean, not a bump in the road. Then, the roads in Michigan for the second half of his life—cracked-spine concrete, potholed, blowing out his alignment, windows shut tight in winter. This was all that Wyatt learned before Mr. Henderson's heart swelled to two times its original size and eventually stopped. A massive, useless organ. Wyatt wished he could have dug deeper past the cars to whatever made a heart swell so big.

After The Best Is Yet to Come, Thunder Blades hired him over the phone. They didn't want experience. They didn't want skill. Blank slates preferred. Lumpy masses of clay to be sculpted into an army of unstoppable salesmen. Wyatt came to know a world of products, each one more amazing than the next. Products, his training stressed, that no one could live without. Products, he realized, he'd been living without. This was surely why he lived alone, why he had no girlfriend or best friend or a close relationship with Mom and Dad. He had dead people's stories, but he needed stuff. Stuff and money. Everything was about money, commission, sale, paycheck, purchase.

By the time the next customer rounds the corner, swinging a

shopping basket merrily, Wyatt has made a nice groove into the head of the sledge. The knives really are amazing. He likes the sound of the knife sawing back and forth, like the sound of old men's labored breathing as they near sleep on a comfortable mattress. He can feel Lee's eyes behind the boxes urging him. *Saw like the wind, Wyatt. Make an impression.* He saws more vigorously, sledge shavings accumulating like a metal blizzard, drifts of dust rising around the head of the sledge.

The customer reaches the cheese display, just before the meat troughs where Wyatt saws. He has messy brown hair and freckles, a dusty face with a thick shadow of stubble. He wears an orange reflective vest over a black T-shirt, asphalt-splotched jeans. A road paver, probably a city worker, the guys who blur past his car windows at the side of the road on his way to work. The customer picks out a quart of small-curd cottage cheese and plunks it into his basket. Then he's on his way, Thunder Blades directly in his path.

Wyatt is lactose intolerant, and watching the man at the cheese display puts him all in knots. It starts in his stomach and creeps into his arms fast at work, now cramping. How long can he last? How long until his arms melt into butter or cream cheese or small curds? How long until the blade goes dull?

Thunder Blades never go dull! Put your trust in the product. A master salesman is filled with faith.

Remembering his training rejuvenates his confidence, gives him a burst of sawing speed. The customer stops, stares, rubs his sandpaper cheeks. Wyatt has captured his attention, is finally doing something right.

We got our hooks in him now. Don't stop. Saw that son-of-a-bitch sledgehammer right in half! If he's impressed now, wait until he sees the rest. Break out the tomatoes!

From the deep pockets of his apron, Wyatt produces a bright-red tomato. He holds it up for the customer, rotates it left and right. It might be the biggest, reddest tomato the man in the orange vest has ever seen. The man scratches his head. He should be explaining what he's about to do, how the blade will still slice with Excalibur sharpness. But his tongue is tar. The words catch like stones in his throat.

Pushing back his nerves, Wyatt slides the serrated blade over the tomato, and it sinks through as if the sledge were nondairy butter. He breathes a sigh of relief. The customer widens his eyes with recognition, nods. Yes, it all makes sense now. The pieces are coming together. These are the best damn knives you'll ever see or want or need.

Back to the sledge. Wyatt is going for a world record with astronomically fast thrusts and pulls of his wrist. Einstein said nothing could move faster than the speed of light, but he was wrong. The passion and pressure fueling Wyatt's thrusts shatter the conventional theories of speed and physics. The shavings shoot out the deepening divot, spilling off the table top and onto the floor, like planets being born from astral dust.

From the opposite direction of the cheese—the seafood side, with the giant tank of plump, mottled brown lobsters—a high-pitched hum approaches. It almost sounds like a song, as if a mermaid might have been plunked into the tank and is trying to sing her way out. It's really quite fantastic, and this distraction causes Wyatt to slip and graze his knuckle—just a scratch, not much blood—but it seeps as bright and ripe as the tomato. He wipes his bloody knuckle on his uniform, under his apron where he hopes no one will see that he's bleeding, that these products can be dangerous. Appearances are important. The customer doesn't notice, because he looks toward the sound, too.

A woman wearing a bright-yellow blouse and black pants hums past his stand, armed with a small vacuum on a slim pole. She sucks up the spilled shavings of Wyatt's salesmanship. After one pass, not a speck remains. She pushes her small vacuum in a full circle around the customer and stops in front of him, propping her elbow on the slim pole, stretching a confident smile. She's small and skinny, has short blonde hair combed over like a school boy. With that tiny body, she could almost be invisible. But she assumes the presence of a greater-sized woman. Every movement—the curve of her wrist, her seductive twists of the tiny vacuum, the slight but unmistakable jut of her hip when she leans—is executed with graceful showmanship.

"Sir, do you wish you had an easier life?" She winks at the customer. "I'm here to make that dream possible. Well, not just me. Our product was envisioned and designed by expert NASA engineers to bring you an out-of-this-world sweeping experience from Warp-Speed Vacuums."

She swoops her hand into her tight pockets and releases a handful of varying-sized gems and gold nuggets. It's amazing so many could fit into such a tight pocket. They sprinkle and bounce across the tile floor. "But Warp-Speed doesn't just handle small messes. It can tackle the heavy-duty work as well."

And then she's at it again, making quick, graceful circles with the tiny vacuum, sucking up each precious stone with a flick of the wrist and a side step here and there. It's a dance. Wyatt is mesmerized. He's forgotten all about the sledge, wondering to himself what heavenly training program blessed her with such a persona and why his hasn't kicked in yet. Perhaps some people are just born with salesmanship talent. She is perfect. He seriously considers upgrading to a new vacuum. But he'd need to sell more knives.

Stay focused on the knives! Don't be taken in by flashy false prophets. There's only room for one miracle product today.

He's back to sawing, stealing a glance as she swoops up the last gem. So perfect. The customer is in awe too. Blood wells up in the cracks of Wyatt's fingers, forming into tiny red tributaries. Maybe the cut is a bit deeper than he first thought. He wipes behind his apron again, hopes nothing shows through, hopes she might keep the customer's attention until his blood coagulates. Damn his blood.

"And just like that, your floors are spotless," she says. "You'll never need to toil away again. Just think of all the time you'll save in cleaning the very biggest of messes to the peskiest specks of insignificant dust."

The customer sets his basket down in order to clap.

Wyatt ponders the last thing she said: insignificant. She was referring to him and his metal shavings. This is not just competition. This is an attack. His stomach burns. Oh God, an ulcer! And no health insurance until he's made one hundred sales or worked six months. He feels sweat build on the crest of his thinning hairline hidden under the poofy chef's hat. His finger bleeds on, and he buries it in his pocket. He's glad his sweat and blood are hidden. Customers want effortlessness. For Wyatt to have a chance here, everything must appear easy.

"But that's not all. Warp-Speed never needs to be emptied. All messes are broken down into their molecular states and exhaust in a refreshing scent of coconut or pine tree fragrance."

Thunder Blades suddenly feel much less miraculous. Her product has molecular innovations by NASA. Their knives are merely designed by some national culinary institute.

A colorful array of fruity Os spills across the floor. Lee must be trying to give him a fighting chance by keeping her busy. Or possibly, he is just as amazed by her miraculous product and wants to see more. Either way, it's a chance for Wyatt to swing the balance of salesmanship back in his power.

He really digs in now, breathing heavily, clattering the knife against the sledgehammer. The customer looks just in time to see an edge of the sledge head disconnect and thud on the floor. Just a slice, but the smallness makes it no less impressive, Wyatt hopes.

The customer lifts his eyebrows and slaps his palms together a few times.

Toucan cereal boxes erupt from the endcap. "See if you can sweep that up, bitch!" Lee says, revealing his secret location.

The woman leans, shifts her weight, rolls her eyes. She walks over to the broken edge of the sledge and slips it into her pocket. Her pants are perfectly fitted, yet somehow she manages to make it disappear just as easily as she produced the gems and nuggets. Wyatt is dumbstruck. All his work gone in a flash, but he doesn't mind so much. He may very well be in love with the small vacuum woman in the yellow blouse. If only they could combine forces.

He imagines an immaculately swept apartment fully stocked with blades that never go dull. Maybe a few toddlers pushing pop-ball vacuums and slicing plastic tomatoes with plastic knives. They'd all go for a drive down smooth California roads, their hearts nearly bursting with joy.

Lee tears open boxes of toucans and flings the contents in furious handfuls. His face is red. His leg juts from his cramped posture into the aisle. Wyatt's guilt overcomes him, seeing Lee flailing from his hiding spot. Lee already has a family, already has teenagers who've grown out of their plastic utensils. Soon they'll be leaving for college and will need real tiny vacuums and perfectly balanced blades. These things require money, which comes from sales, which come from Lee's salesmen, whom Wyatt is one of. Maybe Lee hasn't been managing so great. Why would he be here adding so much pressure to Wyatt's first day? Why is his face so red, the silky hairs above his ears fraying violently in all directions?

From behind Wyatt's stand, he hears cellophane rustle and Styrofoam squeak. He turns to see a ripple of packaged steaks in the refrigerated trough. The steaks erupt, and a large woman in an even yellower blouse pops up. "Fuck you, Lee!" She hurls a T-bone at Lee, who can't move from his cramped hiding spot and takes the meat right across the face. "He's our sale now. Get over it."

"You vulture!" Lee squirms, makes some progress, and slides onto the floor like a walrus. "Candy Walton, I should have known you were behind this. When will you stop scavenging our sales?"

Wyatt wonders about their history, whether Lee was once in his position, enchanted by the beauty and grace of the competition, enticed into an affair. He imagines Lee and Candy in a dark motel room kissing passionately. But this is unpleasant, so he skips to the morning after, when their large sweaty bodies touch again in the morning light and recognition of their huge mistake sets in.

Why take chances with your satisfaction? Only Thunder Blades offers a risk-free trial.

The customer looks nervous now, caught in the middle of fiery competition. He sways to the left, but the small woman in yellow pushes the vacuum in front of him, leaving all in her path sparkling and smelling of coconut. He sways to the right, and she's there again. Spotless floors block his escape.

"Give 'em hell, Wyatt." Lee hurls a box of toucans at Candy but misses, just before she tackles him. "Use the shearing scissors!" he cries, writhing on the tile floor.

Of course, Lee is right. The shearing scissors would be best with their ergonomic handle and deadeye accuracy. But releasing this astounding product so early in the sales pitch is not only radical to his traditional training. It would also be cruel to the saleswoman, who probably needs the money as much as he does. She's just trying to vacuum out a place in this cold world.

"What are you waiting for? Don't hold back now." Lee tosses him the steak that had hit him in the face.

Loyalty comes first. Lee's children. Wyatt's training. Wyatt tears away the cellophane and Styrofoam. He holds the flank of what was once a cow, and it bleeds in his grip, staining his white sleeve. He no longer must hide his own bleeding finger. The cow's blood fuses with his own. He imagines this cow mawing lazily on its cud in an open pasture beside a Michigan freeway, cars zooming past with the windows up. The cow never had to worry about sales pitches or jarred alignment or the products it needed to sell itself. Cows sell well as is.

He raises the scissors. The small woman looks at him, jutting that hip slightly, waiting. He looks back at her, tries to express with his eyes that he's sorry it has come to this. He cuts into the meat, marveling at the control of the twin blades. If only the man in the orange vest could feel how the ergo grips anticipate the shape of his callused skin, welcome his touch, how the hours of shoveling asphalt would melt away. Wyatt wishes the customer stood in his place thinking roadworker thoughts. Wyatt thinks nursing home thoughts. The roadworker would've liked to have heard about roads. He might have cared to listen, might have been able to help.

He slices, snips. Chunks of meat plop in all directions. The tiny vacuum darts after each bloody piece. Sweat builds in tiny dots along the woman's blonde hairline. The customer flicks a piece of meat off his boot, hops back to dodge another.

The results are undeniable now.

Candy lifts herself from the tile floor, kicking away Lee's grabs at her ankles. She pulls two retractable tiny vacuums from black holsters around her hips. "No job too messy for NASA innovation!" She pushes one in each hand, aiding her saleswoman.

Lee trots to Wyatt's side. "Can you believe this?" he huffs, spouting testimonial, wringing his hands at the customer. "I never thought meat preparation could be *so* easy. With Thor's Mighty Shearing Scissors, you'll never have to worry about dangerous fats and gristle again."

Wyatt tries to stay focused on the flesh in his hands. He whittles from the mass of flesh. The meat in his hands, in the blades of the scissors, starts to form two fat arcs on the top, funneling to a point—a heart. But not a heart like the one in elderly Henderson's weak ribs with ventricles and aortas and tangles of swelled junctions. This heart is simpler, like on a Valentine's card, voluptuous and vibrantly red.

You can't make a sale without putting your heart into it.

Lee leans in toward Wyatt's shoulder and speaks through the side of his mouth. "What are you doing? Stick to the protocol. You'll lose your ass trying to get so fancy."

But Wyatt can't stop at this point. Protocol obliterated. There's no turning back. He looks up and sees all eyes on him—the customer dangling his basket, Candy swooping two vacuums in his direction, and the small woman with the blonde hair. She gazes at him with an inquisitive twist of her hips. They all look at him, not the knives. The knives he should be pushing.

When faith falters, trust thyself.

"You're pretty good with those scissors." The customer speaks for the first time. He steps across the polished floors, his boots leaving ghostly prints behind. "How did you do that?"

How could he explain? Looking in the roadworker's eyes, Wyatt sees an appreciation, as if the skilled cuts with his scissors led somewhere real or maybe helped smooth the way, as the constant filling and refilling of potholes does.

Lee steps in between the man and Wyatt. "Anyone could accomplish such a feat with the power of Thunder Blades."

"But I really don't want to. I don't need new knives or a vacuum, but, damn, you all sure put on quite a show for some guy like me."

Candy and Lee crowd the man, telling him about four easy payments, free shipping and handling, then three payments, doubling his order, tripling his order. They pile boxes of amazing products next to his asphalt-scabbed boots. He slides his hands into his pockets and listens, smiling politely. Wyatt doesn't think he'll buy a thing. He wonders about this man's home. His dull steak knives, fast-food wrappers, a push broom with a broken handle. He goes to work, fixes roads, comes home, and is satisfied with less than miraculous. His roads do what they need to do, despite their potholes. They get people places.

While Candy and Lee chatter, the small woman nears the Thunder Blades stand and plants her delicate fingers on the cutting board. Wyatt still holds the heart sculpted from cow. It almost feels like it pumps and thumps.

"That *is* something I've never seen before," she says, shifting her hip. "Must be some training program you guys have."

"I'm learning still," Wyatt says.

She seems impressed. Maybe he's not such a terrible salesman after all.

"Can I hold it?"

Wyatt places his heart into the woman's hands, her soft-looking palms. Droplets of cow blood run down her thin fingers. Maybe it's his blood. She drops the heart to the floor and zooms the vacuum over it. The vacuum struggles at first, clogging, but sucks it through, and a large plume of coconut scent exhales. She wipes the blood on her hand across the outside of Wyatt's white apron, which has been covering the pocks and slashes he's hidden all day.

ONE-HUNDRED-KNUCKLED FIST

WE TORE UP THE EARTH IN THE YARD OF A THREE-STORY FOUR-thousand-square-footer in Swinging Willow subdivision. We backhoed a gash through the silky sod, brown like a week-old scab, red at the center. That hole in the Glavine family's front lawn was a big dig, so deep it split us into pieces, and we were never right again.

We were making a fountain, the Glavines willing to shell out fifteen grand to piddle a Zen waterfall down their front lawn's downgrade, to sparkle diamonds in their eyes from the big bay window large as the sky. They could've just looked outside from seven to five and seen our half-dozen torsos, bare chests gleaming sweat, pocked with clay.

Because we dug earth, because we heaved shovels, because we hauled it away in the back of Rex's not-so-shiny '92 Dodge Ram, our skin never stopped sparkling. We couldn't tear away enough layers to cool down. No one works harder than the hardscaping boys. Won't catch us snipping copper and tugging carpet and swinging brushes inside an air-conditioned house.

We chunked twelve tons out of the ground, dropped ten tons of polished granite and slate back in. Tommy was helping Al set the schedule 40 lines, when Tommy said, "I'd rather be laying ass than laying brass." We boys laughed, because it sounded nice, even though every line was PVC and Tommy didn't know shit about plumbing. That's why three weeks ago the boss had hired Al, a career pipe bender. No more houses for him after they stopped digging foundations in the subdivisions and started planting foreclosure signs. Now he was ours. We liked him and his toolboxes full of purple primers and chamfer cones and the way he could pour hot sand in a pipe and make it bend like magic. We liked how he knew everything about making water flow.

Tommy stood up from the lines and cracked his neck. "Can't wait to get home. Gonna fuck Silvy from behind until Saturday morning," he said, as he announced every Friday. "Who you fucking tonight, boss?"

"I'm fucking serious," Stas, the boss, said, and then pivoted a two-man rose stone toward the sun. "Serious about finishing this fountain before dark, so let's see you all start busting ass."

"Who you fucking, Al?" Tommy said. "One of them tight and crazy Betties from the bar? Take her home and slip that pretty piece of yours between her thighs."

"I don't fuck Betties. I fuck Bobs," Al said, bowed over one of his last pipe seams.

"A butt fucker, eh?" Tommy thrust his pelvis in the air, paddled his invisible lover with a slate shard. "A genuine cocksucker."

We all held our breath, tried not to look at Tommy's mouth, the words spilling past that one veneered tooth that flickered like new PVC. And we didn't look at Al, afraid of how far down to the bottom of the fountain he was, all by himself down there.

"Did you know you hired such a fancy boy, boss?"

"I did not, Tommy," Stas flipped open his phone, clicked it shut. "But now I know at least one of you assholes can oversee design with me."

"Man sauce makes a body strong," Tommy said, "gives you an eye for aesthetics." He kicked some Mexican River Rock pebbles at Al, who kept his head down, laser focused on his chemical weld. "And look here. Ain't two pieces of pipe he don't know how to couple, it appears."

Al flung one of the pebbles back at Tommy's gut. "Couldn't have done it without you," Al said. "Now get down here and hold your end of the pipe, like a good bear."

"Don't try to pretend like that's the end of the shit I'm gonna give you. You've been keeping sexy secrets from Tommy. I have weeks to make up for."

Down in the trench with Al, Tommy kept at it until lunchtime, cussing and coaxing while he held pipe and passed tools. We stayed close, heaved chunks of granite around the dry hole. Not because Al needed us or a wall, but because we had work. Money to make, wives and girlfriends and child support and parole officers. We dumped wheelbarrows of River Rock over backhoe teeth marks. After Tommy's cum-guzzling jokes hit a dozen, they sounded the same as any other. Sounded the same as when Tommy talked about the tight pink kitty between Stas's twenty-two-year-old honey's legs, or when Tommy said nothing beat getting a BJ while he took a shit, or how Rex's favorite hooker told him his foreskin smelled like blue cheese. It was just work. Al laid pipe and rigged the pump, and we heaved boulders.

But Rex stayed silent, didn't laugh, didn't act out Tommy's words waving his wire strippers in front of his crotch like he usually did. Some current crossed inside him, shorted his nerves until his tongue mangled into a mute lump. Rex used to be a union electrician, until his union folded. Now the closest he came to his old trade was wiring up the fountain pump. Boring to a wire snipper who used to diddle the guts of x-ray machines, wattage that could broil intestines.

We thought maybe Rex was just pissed about the glitch in the pump that kept the fountain silent as his mouth. Rex kept his head down, digging through the dirt to find the lost connection. Once Al finished his perfect lines, he tried to help, dug alongside Rex with a scrap piece of pipe. He was standing behind Rex's bent waist, plowing with his schedule 40, when Tommy said, "Looks like Rex is curious. Give him a few thrusts and see if he likes it."

Rex jumped up, knocked Al's pipe clinking to the pebble bed.

Their shirtless bellies collided in Rex's attempt to scuttle out of the hole, and that got Tommy going even worse. We tried not to laugh, but we couldn't help it when Rex tripped over the outcropping, ran to his shirt, crumpled and baking in the sun, yanked it over his hairy back. His fat lips twisted over his clenched teeth.

Rex slunk to his truck. He sat in the cab for the next two hours, his cell phone jammed against his ear, his mouth still unmoving. Close to quitting time, he headed back to the yard and stabbed his spade into the pebble bed, into the dirt beneath, as if he were hunting magma. He dug hard and deep, shoving elbow and swinging fist. None of us dared go near him. We moved up the fountain, dodging flung pebbles. His gray shirt darkened to sweat-black.

We hauled in the last of the two-man granites. Each cost more than we would earn that day. Rocks too smooth for proper grip. Rocks variegated with bolts of pink quartz and sparkles of blue and green. Rocks that sucked sweat from our hands. We carried in twos up the downgrade, shoulders leaning toward our partners, foreheads pulled together under the weight. An assembly line of shirtless hardscapers. Stas jerked and budged, adjusted each boulder a quarter inch here and there, didn't ask Al for his aesthetic opinion, didn't ask any of us, same as any other gig. And Tommy ran out of jokes, as he always did, his jaw tired as our arms. But Rex kept digging deeper into the gash in the earth filled with slate steppers and pebbles and boulders and shirtless men and Al.

Just before we finished sprinkling the rest of the Mexican River Rocks, before the sun turned purple and then smashed into dusk, Rex gave up digging. He paced the fountain, stopped at the top, and leaned against one of Stas's perfectly adjusted rose rock boulders. The dying sun lit up the pinks, cast Rex's crinkled forehead in purples. We smoked cigarettes on the sod while Al recoupled the flex lines. It was the last touch of the gig, something only Al knew how to do, so we waited. Waited until Rex winked at Tommy, aimed the point of his spade down at Al. Rex said to Tommy, "Here's a way to make a fag rock hard." Then Rex pushed the rose rock, a two-man boulder disturbed by one man. Tommy ran toward Rex.

We exhaled smoke in their direction, our bodies lurching. But we couldn't stop falling rocks. No one can.

We heard the smacks, the sickening sound of a two-hundred-dollar rock snapping slate shards, busting itself into useless fragments. Al held his glued flex too long, jumped too late. Rose rock careened, a deadened landing on shin. Snap of bone or rock. And then Tommy was gripping Rex's collar. The torn cotton shrieked. Rex laughed, scanned our faces, waited for us to join. He kept laughing when Tommy shoved him to the ground, kicked him in the kidney. And Tommy, our joker, he couldn't stop the laughs. Couldn't silence silent Rex. We bit through our filters, dropped our cherries onto the pristine sod.

Al crawled out of the pebble bed, and it was then that we saw the dark around his left shin. Blood. Stone blood from Rex's rock. The two-man, two-days'-pay rock that smashed into worthless shards.

We wanted to lift him, haul his broken body. That's what we knew how to do. But that seemed stupid now. Al sucked air and squinted up at us through the burned-out dusk. We wished we knew how to handle him, didn't want to give him to some EMT kid who could lift that rock-bleeding leg. Stas fumbled for his cell phone, dropped it into the fountain. The phone clacked, battery popping out and disappearing into crag shadows. We dug through our pockets, through sweat-soaked denim for our own explodable phones. All but Tommy. Only he knew how to touch broken Al. He reached out his hand, interlaced fingers, pulled. Tommy heaved Al's arm over his bare shoulders and lugged him to his Honda Civic, the smallest car for the biggest guy on our crew. Panels scratched, front door dented from that night when Tommy drank too much and had to slam an even bigger man's head into the door. His piece-of-shit car whined and gurgled every morning before the sun eked up over the sod of the suburbs. But on this night, Tommy's Honda glimmered as it serpentined out of the cul-de-sac.

We slept restlessly, next to snoring wives and silent girlfriends and all alone. We rolled into the divot of worn-out springs, dreamed of suffocation, reawoke. Where was Rex tonight? Still driving his rusty Dodge, afraid to pull into his driveway, beside the lawn we had no hand in sodding or seeding?

On one of our dozen trips out of bed, hands fumbling against leaden shadows where we knew there was once a light switch, we gave up, slid down the wall to a squat. We couldn't bring on quiet dreams by jerking off or drinking milk or chewing two o'clock salami sandwiches. We carried our cell phones in the waistband of our underwear, waiting for a call. On his way home, Stas bought a new phone at the shop next to the hospital where Tommy and Al sit in the emergency waiting room. No insurance, so no rush. Stone blood hardly life threatening. Stitches and tetanus needles, some bandages cleaner than Tommy's sweat-hardened T-shirt wrapped tight around Al's shin. An x-ray and some valium in waiting. Waiting for results, for the bright-white bone sparking across black film. Waiting with Tommy, who keeps patting Al's back, asking if there's someone he should call. Parents? Sisters or brothers? Tommy's hand circles around Al's shoulder blades, across muscles tense and taut like his own. He pulls his hand away when the old man across the room turns his one good eye toward him, the other hidden behind a handful of bunched-up white panties stained with brown-dried blood.

No, no one, Al says through his teeth.

Your boyfriend? Tommy whispers, and thinks of denim crotches pressing together, can't find the joke that should be there.

No boyfriend, Al says. Don't bother him with this shit.

And Tommy thinks of the time he smashed that bigger man's head into his door panel, which was after Tommy called that bigger man a fag at the bar. Just a joke, like at work, but the bigger man didn't get it like his rock-slinging boys. They always got it. Until Rex didn't. And that bigger man at the bar wouldn't stop shoving and swinging until Tommy clunked skull to metal. He wonders if that bigger man told his wife that night. Tommy wouldn't tell those jokes outside work no more. Tommy didn't tell his old lady he dented his car with a skull that night, and they didn't fuck from behind like she likes. He said he was too tired, and she just flicked off the lamp. But he felt her staring all night.

Tommy pours coffee for Al into a chipped Styrofoam cup. Al takes a sip, passes it back. And it's probably burned, cooked on the hot plate for the last six hours, but it smells good, like earth and warm, and the emergency room air-conditioning is blowing hard. Not like the comfort of sweat, of day, of lawns and stones, of hauling rocks and spreading sod with his boys, with us, who want to be us, but we can't find the light switch and can't get to sleep because we're wondering about Tommy and Al and Rex. We hate that old man and his bleeding eye and his bunched-up panties who won't stop glaring at Tommy even though his good eye probably isn't worth a shit, all pale and milky.

But Tommy forgets about him, and the old man turns as invisible as the crinkled fashion magazine under his seat, opened up to a spread on bikini season where a page has been torn away, stashed into the pants of an eleven-year-old who was waiting for its mama to get her blackened, busted-up eye sewn for the twenty-second time. Tommy takes a sip, puts his lips where Al's pressed, and it doesn't mean a damn thing to Tommy. We finally fall asleep.

We got to the fountain early, before sun, full of coffee and nicotine, sitting in our running cars and waiting to see who showed. We twisted the radio knob, skipped past morning shows, one DJ's belching laugh bleeding into the next one's. We rechecked our phones, cycled through missed calls, but there was nothing missed from missing Tommy and Al and Rex. And what if Rex showed? We gripped our steering wheels, dirt-crusted nails digging into rubber.

Boss Stas arrived late for the first time ever. He stepped out of his truck, phone pinched between ear and shoulder. His neck looked broken through our rearview mirrors. We got out to steal the words he hummed into the receiver: "Sorry, honey. We'll get new rocks. I need them for this gig. No. No word from the guys yet." Nothing that told us everything we wanted to know.

Stas cracked his tailgate, and inside was a stack of slate steppers and one two-man rose rock, a rock like any other rock. Like the rock that stomped Al's shin. Like the rock we wanted to toss into the gash of earth after Rex crawled inside, and we would close our eyes and say a joke like a prayer. But this rock wasn't like any other. It blazed up all kinds of quartz and sparkle. This rock was Stas's young old lady's cherry-picked perfect rock, transplanted from his own home.

Stas climbed onto his truck bed, leaned into the rose rock, budged it inch by inch, rock screaming against steel. He worked it to the edge, and then we cradled it. That two-man rock turned into a many-man rock, and we carried it all the way up the downgrade, to the gap-toothed outcropping.

The cul-de-sac rattled, backfired. Tommy's Honda swerved down the blacktop, squealed to a stop behind Stas's scraped tailgate. Al exited Tommy's Honda, rapped on the hood, hollered, "Not done yet, boys?"

Tommy slid out next, and the two of them staggered up the downgrade. Al wore yesterday's jeans but with the right leg hacked to thigh. And we were all wearing yesterday's jeans, because there's no point washing away the sweat we'd make again today and tomorrow. A bright-white cast wrapped his leg where the jeans were missing. Tommy and Al grinned like motherfuckers, reeked like Friday's shots lined across the bar.

"Are you two drunk?" Stas gripped Al's shoulder.

"What else do you do after getting out of the emergency room at four in the morning?" Tommy kicked at the new rose rock. It stayed put like it'd always been there.

We burned through the morning, replacing the chipped slate, careful not to shift every other stone, topple our precious puzzle. Every rock, pretty side up for the ugliest boys in town, shucked shirts and smeared dirt and beer guts and Tommy's appendicitis scar winking like a stab wound. The only thing to worry about was Rex's Dodge popping through the houseline. But he didn't show, and he never did find that lost connection. Tommy found the frayed wire by chance, between him and Al betting quarters on where that son-of-a-bitch splice could be. Al slapped the quarter in Tommy's palm while we filled the fountain bed, diluted Al's blood that was down there somewhere, dried and brown, now drowned. By lunchtime, the drunk was mostly worn off of our missing boys, and they recoupled the last of the flex.

Stas fired up the fountain, and it pissed a perfect stream. Tommy stood barefoot in the middle of our new steppers. He swayed, but our rocks didn't. Solid like one hundred knuckles packed into a single giant fist.

SAWDUST AND GLUE

WHILE WE'RE TAKING LUNCH WITH THE PAINTERS, MY SON
Ramon tells Big Dave his job is easier than ours. Something you
don't say to any workingman and certainly not to Big Dave. When I
was a twenty-three-year-old dumbshit like Ramon, I sat down with
my crew at a Denny's for an 8:00 p.m. Moons over My Hammy,
after a ten-hour day of framing. A scraggly bearded Mexican
bussed our table, and I told him not to strain himself carrying
dishes for real workingmen. My crew laughed through two more
coffee refills and three more cigarettes that we smothered into
our empty mugs. That Mexican ambushed me in the parking lot,
busted one of my teeth. I landed a jab on his right eye, kicked
his gut when he fell. I got in my truck and drove home, and that
guy went back to work.

But he was small. Big Dave is not. And now Ramon is so worked
up he can't hit a shiner with his nail set, keeps slipping and pounding deeper holes into the baseboard. It'd be painful to listen to him
cracking through the wood, except it's particleboard. All sawdust
and glue mitered together to look like nice houses instead of the
cookie-cutter junk that fills the subdivision. I haven't sunk a nail
through the grain of oak or cherry in over a year. Sometimes I
imagine all the good trees have been used up.

"Maybe," Ramon says to the baseboard, "Big Dave won't come back to the sub if it's raining."

"That could be." I look through my window trim at gray clouds rolling over the fresh shingles across the street.

"Maybe Big Dave's so big he's scared of storms. So big he gets hit by lightning."

Thunder rattles the panes. Instead of lightning, Big Dave jumps in front of the window. A thin layer of glass separates our faces. He's painting trim outside while we put it together inside. Big Dave and I stare at the same wall on our respective sides, would be shaking hands if not for the Sheetrock and studs and siding between us.

Ramon is right about Big Dave being big. Big Dave's arms are so wide they split shirtsleeves, we guess, because we've never seen him wear sleeves. I feel my trim shake against the pressure of his mashing brushstrokes. Big Dave's so big he can't find a pair of pants that fit him, flashing ass crack when he bends to jam his four-inch barn brush into the cutting pot. And Big Dave's so tough he chews a bent nail to help him quit smoking. I see it through the window, flickering between his lips. The flicker disappears, and since I don't see him spit the nail out, I'm pretty sure he swallowed it, has a stomach like a porcupine.

"I'll just stay out of sight." Ramon doesn't look our way. I hear him rip another hole through the base. "Give him time to cool down and deal with it tomorrow."

"What will you do tomorrow?" I watch Big Dave bite off a few bent bristles from his brush.

There's always tomorrow, another house, another quarter-acre plot, another slippery tentacle of cookie cutters made of plastic and glue and vinyl, so little metal and wood like the old days, when I was doing renovations and Ramon's mama, Joni, was changing his diapers. Ramon used to chew up the handles on my tools. Ramon's mama didn't like that, and I didn't like his spit rusting up my good hammer. Joni punched me one night, drove my jagged tooth through my lip, after I slapped a Stanley measuring tape out of Ramon's mouth. I didn't last much longer as a father after that night.

Now Ramon has got two kids he never sees, two grandkids as imaginary to me as pink ivory wood. Judge wouldn't even dare an every-other-weekend situation. He has child support to pay, a background that'll never check out clean since he got busted with a one-cook two-liter bottle for meth snuggled into his kid's empty car seat. Then there're the bullshit anger-management classes for biting that cop's neck after they cuffed him. That's what Joni told me the newspaper said the next day, but they exaggerate. Ramon has always been small, was a quiet and shy kid when I had him on my weekends. Now construction is the only job he can get, and I'm the only dope who would hire him. I needed someone reliable, someone I could count on every day, and he has proven to be a decent nail bender for the last three weeks. And Ramon needs me, this job, his last option.

Ramon rises from the corner and stretches his back. Big Dave spots him through the window and stabs the butt of his brush against the pane. He gives Ramon the finger, but since Ramon doesn't see it, I'm the one who has to face that giant finger pressed against the glass.

"You shouldn't have talked shit about the painters," I say.

Telling Ramon what he shouldn't have done today is as useless as when I told him last week that he shouldn't mix making babies and making meth. I apologize to Ramon for that one by nailing my window casing home, filling the silent room with the roar of the compressor that drowns out Big Dave's knocking. Once the compressor dies out, Big Dave has disappeared. The window shows nothing but gray clouds bunched together like knuckles.

"That stupid asshole just swings his brush around out there," Ramon says. "You gotta agree they got the easiest job in the sub. Anyone can push paint."

The front-door handle rattles, and then the door booms, someone kicking outside.

"Why'd you lock the front door?" I say.

"Let's keep working. Maybe he'll just piss off."

Locked doors are for homeowners. Seven to seven, these doors are open to anyone lugging a tool. So I open up, and Big Dave fills the threshold, hands full of rollers and brushes, sandpaper strips curling out his pockets, gallon cans hanging from each pinkie. His eyebrows look like they're trying to collide, creases in his forehead small rodents could hide inside.

"Should have known it was the Smiley crew," Big Dave says. "Locking up so you can take naps in the closets?"

And, yes, I named my business Smiley Carpentry, because that's my name and it sounds friendly. Smiley guys are the type of guys you let in your house, maybe even leave them a spare key. But, no, I've never napped in a closet, and every one of my guys I caught sleeping in a closet got sent home permanently to sleep in his own bed. That's the good thing about Ramon. He never sleeps, out late every night and still can swing hammer for fourteen hours. Even when he's in bed, he growl-snores all night through my paper-thin apartment walls. I don't let myself worry. Smiley Carpentry will work out for him, and he'll have his own place and real sleep soon.

Big Dave stomps toward Ramon, and Ramon shrinks back to the base, smacking away, pretending he didn't notice anyone come in. Big Dave plunks his paint cans behind Ramon, and Ramon flinches each time one drops on the OSB. We pop nails and buzz trim all day. He should be plenty used to loud noises.

"Hey, Dave," Ramon says, when he finally pivots around to face him, "I was just setting the shiners for you."

"Should I thank you for doing your job?"

Ramon laughs, and I shoot a few more nails home, make sure to leave the heads gleaming. "We'll be out of here in a few hours," I tell Big Dave. "And then you can get to painting."

"That's all right." He digs his canine into a can of nail filler and cracks it open. "I don't mind getting chummy with the hardest-working guys in the sub."

"I never said we worked the hardest," Ramon says, but gets cut off when Big Dave starts whistling. I think it's a Rush song. We need to buy a radio. A silent house is a tryout for the amateur talent show. Big Dave whistles through a whole set list, not unlike what

I'm sure is playing in the other houses: more Rush, Steve Miller Band, AC/DC. He hits the high notes so loud I expect the contact cement to curdle and the laminate on the counters to curl. I pop out twice as many nails as the trim needs, just so the compressor kicks on more often. I cut each board twice, three times, four. Big Dave whistles through the compressor rumble, syncs his notes with the saw's whine, as if I'm his backup.

Ramon sings along. Quiet and falsetto. Ramon is trying to make nice. My, sir, you might not work as hard as a Smiley, but your whistling is infectious.

I finally head upstairs and leave the lovebirds to jam it out. I'm only up there an hour before I hear Ramon yelling. He has a high and light singing voice, but he roars like someone punched nails through his spine. Now I know why his neighbors in his wife's apartment complex phoned the cops. It must've sounded like a bear loosed in Ramon's unit when they called in those domestics. I never believed he really had it in him. My skinny kid. Even a small Smiley T-shirt looks too big on him.

I hustle downstairs and Ramon is covered in white primer. He stands in the middle of the room, arms outstretched, eyes closed, chest heaving. Some fancy breathing pose he learned in anger management. The primer drips from the hem of Ramon's shorts and tap-taps against the subfloor. Big Dave smirks, and Ramon's face glows red against the primer. He shakes his finger at Big Dave's cleft chin, and Big Dave bites at it. I wouldn't be surprised if Big Dave's diet consisted of carpenters' fingers. Ramon crams his finger into a fist, says, "Five thirty, in the middle of the cul-de-sac, I'm gonna rip your ass off."

I wish people would choose their threats more carefully. That's the heat of anger. And, I don't know, maybe someone could rip an ass off. Maybe Ramon has done it. Maybe his teenage bedroom in his mama's basement was lined with torn asses, hung on his wall like bearskins. I wasn't around for that, wouldn't know.

"You got it," Big Dave says, and then swipes up all his tools in the curls of his fingers, jangling them along as he moseys out the front door. Ramon kicks the primer can, splatters the last of its paint against the wall. He grits his teeth, flashing his perfectly straight incisors that I spent all that child support on. Joni thought a nice smile would help him in life, but his name's not even Smiley. He changed it to his mama's name when he was fourteen. Ramon Bayer. Anyway, I did okay with my chipped tooth.

Ramon slaps his forehead, pulls back his hair, which is already thinner than my own. They say a kid gets his hairline from his mother's side. A father shouldn't ever have to see his son go bald first. I buzz a few baseboards through the saw to give him time to stew.

He shakes his hands out, and a few strands of his hair flutter to the OSB, where they'll be covered with carpet next week, under homeowner toes in a month, and then for however long it takes a family to grow.

"Now would be a good time to cut out early," I say to the saw.

"You were right about tomorrow. I'd still have to deal with him then." Ramon slips the primer-drenched Smiley shirt over his head. It slaps wetly against the OSB. Ramon kicks at the pile of shirt, and there's my logo, smiling mouth now crinkled into a grimace, looking up at me like a ghost through all that white. Ramon's bare torso is so thin, as if God ran him through the planer. "Fuck assertive problem solving. I'm gonna fight that bastard."

I head out to the van and open the back door. Above the scrap particleboard, I keep a shelf full of Smiley shirts. It used to be full. Now there's one left, and it's an XXL. I never found anyone to work for me who would fill out that size, even though most of them ask for a shirt one size too big. Everyone pretends they're bigger than they are, and they end up looking smaller, buried in their too-large shirts. That's probably why Big Dave can't find any clothes his size. All those guys wishing for bigger, and all the big guys wishing they could find a shirt that fits.

Back inside the house, Ramon snaps a piece of casing over his knee. He busts it in half and then picks up one of the halves and busts that one over his knee, too. The shards of casing get so small

I think it will be impossible for him to break another, but he does. Ramon is hiding strength in those spidery hands, that bony knee. I throw the XXL over his shoulder.

He pulls the shirt on, and the hem lines his kneecaps. It looks like a dress on my son. He looks like a child, like when he was five and Joni bought him Superman and the Incredible Hulk pajamas. He never wore them, preferred my old work shirts reeking of dried sweat and sawdust. I used to think he'd grow up to be a fine carpenter. Joni wanted him to wear cute pajamas, to go to college, become a lawyer or something like that. She couldn't even afford a lawyer when Ramon got busted with blow back in high school.

"Dave's not so big," Ramon says, looking out the window. The oversized Smiley logo on his back flashes an absurdly wide grin at me. "And he sucks at his easy job."

I look out the window, too. Big Dave's in front of the house across the street, where one of the other painters has straddled his shoulders and is reaching up to slap white on the top of a porch column. Dave's pushing a roller up to the other guy's cut. It's quite a sight, this two-headed smattering of white paint, Big Dave getting bigger and smarter, hurrying to beat the rain that's surely coming now. The sky is nearly black, though not a drop has fallen.

"He's a better ladder than a painter," Ramon says.

Ramon never sat on my shoulders. My back is all kinks and spurs. On his sixth birthday, I took him to the zoo. This other kid was sitting on his dad's shoulders so he could get a closer look at some tamarin monkeys perched on a tree branch. Ramon asked to sit on my shoulders, and I pretended I couldn't hear him. It was either that or explain to my kid that the job his dad did, the one he wanted to slip into like his Smiley-shirt pajamas, had warped his spine into a hook. Then that kid on his dad's shoulders screamed. The tamarins had snatched a fistful of this kid's hair through the fence and wouldn't let go. The dad tried to reach up and wrestle the monkey's pencil-thin arm. He couldn't reach, just flailed his arms at that tiny monkey. I smiled to Ramon, but he looked worried, like he wanted to help. That's what they get for being stupid, underestimating that monkey just because he looked like a fluffy toy. He was still in a cage. They only put wild things in cages.

Ramon lugs a stack of base upstairs, and I should follow him. But I linger at the window, keep my eye on Big Dave spreading white, making those fat porch columns glare against the black sky. Ramon pounds up and down the stairs, dropping off base with pencil lines scratched where he wants me to miter. I do this for him. I cut his boards quick so he always has something to nail, work to keep his mind off quitting time.

The sky punctuates five o'clock by ripping a thunderclap that rattles the windows. I answer the sky by shooting my last nail home. It's nice when we finish a house at the end of a day, but it means little since there's always more to do, since there's Big Dave outside my window boxing the first fat drops of rain. He swings high and heavy, jabs low, obliterating the drops before they touch ground. It feels like Big Dave's sparring shakes the whole house, but it's just the thunder. The other painters scurry around him, stretching masking plastic around the porch columns so they won't get wet. A loose piece of plastic blows away. Big Dave uppercuts his sledge of a fist at the plastic, and I imagine the plastic smashing into pieces, reverting back to oil and splashing onto the tarvy. His blow hardly makes a difference, the plastic so light, and it floats upward, over the houses, into the road and then the cornfields. Might not stop until it strangles a crow pecking a rotting husk or until it finds another road, plasters itself across a windshield, and sends a car hurtling into a ditch.

Ramon creaks upstairs, double-checking our work. I pop a squat on the stairs and wait. There's no rush. And maybe Ramon will diddle around up there all night, do some meditative breathing, skip his date with Big Dave. But Ramon hops down the stairs, his oversized shirt flouncing around his thighs. "Ready to go, Pap?"

"Big Dave's still out front. Slip out the back and cut through the cornfields. I'll pick you up in the van."

He approaches the window, runs his fingers over our casing.

Lightning flickers against his pale skin, and I wait for the next big boom to tell me how far off the real storm is.

"Those are some tight miters. Could hardly fit any of Big Dave's caulk in there." Ramon thumbs my cut, the casing he nailed. "Wish he'd recognize the kind of work we do, how we make their job easier."

"It's junk particleboard. Doesn't mean much."

"Let's go see that big fucker," he says, and his back is the hugest Smiley I've ever seen sliding through the front door.

I step on the van's gas once Fondly Lane comes into view, but Ramon points a scabbed finger left instead of right. To the cul-de-sac instead of the exit for the subdivision, where Fondly Lane turns onto 43, where a real road with a number could take us home.

"We did that one, and now someone's living there," Ramon says, nodding at a ranch with green siding. "What other ones did you do on this street?"

"All of them."

If I straightened out all the hallways and rooms, merged the window frames and door jambs and baseboards, into one straight line, how far would it go? All the way to Oklahoma, where Ramon spread his mama's ashes two months ago? Farther, I bet. If it went straight down through the cemetery where Joni and I bought two plots when we weren't more than kids, that endless line of trim would make it all the way to the molten center of earth, and then on and on and on. Hell is a hallway of trim that never ends. When my back gives out, Ramon will step over my collapsed shoulders and go right on sawing and nailing. I won't find an end, and if my son ever gets there, he'll have to go back to the beginning and set all our shiners.

No one lives in any of the five houses surrounding the cul-de-sac. They aren't selling this deep in the sub yet. Big Dave is waiting in the rain, five other painters, some electricians and plumbers, the garage-door installer. They've formed a half circle around Big Dave, who's stretching his arms behind his back.

"There's nothing to prove here," I say.

Ramon pops open the door. I hop out and follow the thinning spot on the back of his head, glistening with sweat or rain. Big Dave jogs in place a little, cracks his knuckles. Ramon tugs the shirt over his head and tosses it to me. His bare toothpick frame makes him look taller, defines each vertebrae knuckling through his skin. Ramon doesn't do any stretches, doesn't grin at me like Big Dave does to his half circle. His chest heaves faster and faster. His spine bounces up and down. I can't hear him because of the rain, but if I could, he'd sound like a cat hissing, a dog growling, some mad animal.

Big Dave finally notices my boy's grinding teeth and gasping lungs. He says, "How cute that both father and son Smiley showed up." He points to his chin. "Go on. I'll make it easy for you and give you a first swing."

Ramon swings so fast he hits Big Dave's finger still pointing at his chin. He swings again, mashes Big Dave's nose. He keeps swinging, stretching his thin arms high as they'll reach to connect with Big Dave's face. Big Dave chuckles between blows, but Ramon shuts him up by digging a knuckle into his teeth. Big Dave probably expected a shoving match, where he'd knock Ramon on his ass and that would be it. They could go to the bar and laugh about it, over a beer and a shot.

That's not what Big Dave gets. Ramon won't hit anywhere else but Big Dave's face, and he doesn't slow down. Big Dave's lips and cheeks swell. He pushes Ramon away, but Ramon keeps on coming. The half circle of guys gawk. They won't step in, and Ramon's fists keep wailing until Big Dave falls sideways, clunks his head on the tarvy. No splash, even with all this rain, because the tarvy guys are good, smoothed their work fine, bowed it just right so no water collects in the middle. No break for Big Dave's huge head, which hits just as the thunder booms again. I forget to check for lightning. I'm watching my boy straddle a huge chest, pound Big Dave's motionless head against tarvy. I'm waiting for Big Dave to spit nails from his belly, to stand up and hurl Ramon onto the freshly shingled roofs.

But that won't happen. Big Dave is big, but Ramon smashed three of his wife's TVs, bit a policeman on the neck, huffed a pint of turpentine when he was fourteen, wore Smiley shirts his whole life and dreamed of sawing wood and pounding nails, and now he growls like a starved wolf.

Ramon stops swinging for a moment, faces me. I don't know if his perfect teeth are smiling or grinding. I run my tongue over my tooth, the broken edge that's dulled down over the years. Ramon's straight teeth look sharp enough to slice his tongue.

I could step in, yank my son off Big Dave before he gets himself into real trouble. Hell, I could just tell him to stop. But it's Ramon's fight, and sometimes a father has to let his kid figure things out on his own. Or sometimes a father is afraid of someone he doesn't recognize. I twist the XXL Smiley shirt in my fists and wish for workers sleeping in closets. That's a problem I can deal with, work easier than watching your son turn into something wild, something made of blood and guts and fire. Joni would have known what to do, but all I can think about is the worthless trim I cut into perfect miters, how when Ramon gets out of jail this time, I won't have any more Smiley shirts left.

CAN PICKING

WE HEAVE CREAKING HEFTY BAGS OVER OUR BACKS. BAGS
that look the size of baby elephants or oily engine blocks. But we
aren't that tough. Bags of dried syrup and spit. And aluminum—
hidden shimmers of red, white, and blue and lime green. Ten cents
a can in Michigan. We got your Cokes and Pepsis and Faygos, your
smuggled Pabsts, and you won't get them back. You kicked them
down the bleachers when State took the lead in the second quarter. You jumped in the air and shrieked. We smoked Winstons on
the tailgate of Murray's F-150 and didn't give a damn about your
cheering, except for the hollow pings and pangs that followed. We
bit our butts to the sound of sprinkling dimes, eyed the exits, and
planned how to best sneak in. Alibi of orphaned umbrella on the
bleachers, lost purse, stranded child.

Now we play the song of rescued treasure. Crinkle, groan, and
crunch when we stuff our bags. Keep it a hum or get caught. A
hundred shuffling cans full of air when we hike down the bleacher
stairs. Dump them and stack them in the back of Murray's rusted
bed. Baby Trudy weighs two hundred pounds and isn't a baby anymore at ten and in a training bra. She jumps off the roof of the
cab, belly flops onto the Hefty bags so we can cram more. Her
daddy, Two-Tooth Linus, is scared she'll smack the rails, ruin her

pretty face. That's all she's got to win a man since her body's so big. Murray's boy, Wilfred, tells him not to worry. Baby Trudy'll make a fine bus driver or bull dyke. Hell, if she keeps growing like that, she could be the bus.

We rest syrup-stained palms on Linus's bunched-up shoulders. Not worth another back-of-the-cruiser joyride. Wilfred is just a baby, even though he's seventeen. Let him be a fool, and let Baby Trudy do her work. She pretends she's having fun, dreams herself away, diving into a rich man's swimming pool. Or maybe a fountain lined with coins, like she did last week, skimming enough coins to earn us a pizza and a case of Coke.

We turned those coins to food, and we'll turn these cans to coins. The money keeps on coming. Until the cleaning crew shows up. We know where they start, over on the west-side bleachers, and we got there first. Half their job done for them. All those cans all gone. Just soggy paper cups and half-eaten hotdogs squishing under their sneakers. Poor students and Latinos working the cleanup shift like suckers for $7.40 an hour. That's seventy-four cans. Nothing. And then the government snags a dozen of their cans. Murray's boy can sneak that into a Hefty in five minutes, and no IRS man'll ever dig his starched cuffs into our sticky bags to count.

We know those cleaners are jealous, so we work faster, smarter, covert, when they show up across the field of groomed grass. We slink beneath the bleachers, blend black like our Hefty bags into the shadows.

Wilfred is fed up with hiding. He pangs up while we tiptoe down. His face gleams in the halide lights, painted like a clown, all white with black eyes, a stretched-out black mouth. He sprints from one can to the next. Wilfred wants us to call him Spike, hates what he calls his slave name, but he's as white as Two-Tooth Linus's snaggle-tooth incisors. His face ain't painted like the can droppers' faces, like those bleacher people's cheeks smeared green and white or blue and yellow. Wilfred doesn't paint his face for the team but for some rap group. Not just music but a revolution, he says. But revolution never comes. We know that from when our granddaddies chucked lug nuts at cops in Flint and the GM factories still closed on us, from the building bust when we pawned our power tools. Nothing changes for good. And the only music that matters is the crunching of an almost-missed can under our boots. It sings to us and then plink-tinkles into the Hefty.

Wilfred is taunting fate, a backtracking race to the top bleachers, where he spies a tallboy sparkling. The sucker cleaners spot him, beep their walkie-talkie. Security men on their way. He don't care, hollers to them that they can't keep him down. They huddle around the talkie, point, and chatter. Bright under the spotlights, Wilfred drops his pants, flops his dick at them, swings his Hefty in the air. And nothing them suckers can do but cower and report.

We know what's coming. We keep our heads down. Bending and plucking. Our Hefty bags bulge, but we keep jamming. No time for no more Baby Trudy drop-offs now. Still so many glints around us. Our fingers not fast enough. A damn shame Wilfred's so dumb. Dropout, spray-can huffer, lanky brain-dead motherfucker. A thirty-bag night fades into a fifteen-bagger.

But we try, rush for what's left. Linus splits his finger on a Mello Yello. Bleeding so much he's dropping cans. We keep going, wait for the bellows of barrel chests, the failed linebackers who now wear navy blue and scurry across the field. They're reliving that last day of glory, that quarterback sack when they made a shinbone snap. They blitz our way, fingering mace and zappers.

Worthless Wilfred already hightailed it back to his daddy's truck. We count down, watch their glowing legs slicing through the bleacher struts. Past the forty, the thirty, twenty-five. Five yards a can, we figure. Maybe ten for Linus and his dripping finger, spouting more now that the blood's pumping. Past the end zone, and that means they'll hunt the bleacher shadows, means quitting time for our seam-splitting Hefties.

We make for the truck. Fast but smooth so we don't jostle our paychecks too much. One hole and we got an aluminum leak. Linus can't keep up, so we sling his bags over our shoulders. To the gates, out the fence, and Murray's got the engine hot in the parking lot.

We peel out, and those security boys'll be left with full mace cans and adrenaline. If only they looked at their feet, saw what we see. We wonder if the cleaners will save those cans or toss them, not worth the time to sort it out. That time of theirs that's hardly worth nothing. We wonder if everyone forgot that promise Michigan made to us: our trash always worth a dime.

In Murray's bed, we grip the rails with one hand, hug our Hefty bags with the other so they won't fall out. Inside the cab, Murray swats Wilfred backside the head, yelling something. Wilfred takes off his shirt and gets to wiping away that paint. Linus finds Baby Trudy faceup, arms and legs spread securely over our bags. She's watching the streetlights whip past like falling stars. He'd stroke her dirty, blonde hair, but one hand's bleeding and the other holds the bags tight.

EVERYTHING A SNAKE NEEDS

WE WEREN'T SUPPOSED TO TOUCH THE SNAKES AT RIZZO'S Reptile Emporium, but I knew Drew was doing it. That was how he earned so many Realm of the Reptiles Bonuses, how he scored Iguana of the Month his first three months in a row. It had nothing to do with his college degree. I'd only graduated high school, but I was smarter. And it wasn't that Drew was a foot taller than me and half my age. Looks and vitality fade. Customers see through that. Reptile expertise was the key to success at Rizzo's, and I had ten years' experience, knew every detail about each product we carried, from the Mojave tank murals to the Ultra-Health Heat Rocks. When he'd started here, I'd thought Drew would be my protégé, someone to take under my wing and mold. I wanted to share everything I had, pass my knowledge like bloodlines. But Drew took the easy way.

I was talking heat lamps with this fourth-grade teacher, telling her how ceramic was the way to go, would outlast glass, distribute tropical temperatures evenly for her classroom's pet turtle. She wanted only the best, and that's what I did. I went to retrieve a lamp from storage, giving a nod to the big sign proclaiming Rizzo's number one rule: DON'T TOUCH THE SNAKES. Rizzo left us this sign in his absence, gone for a week at the International Repti-Mania Conference, leaving me in charge. Me and the sign.

When I returned to the showroom, the teacher was gone. I scanned the aisles from the front of the store. The evening sun bled orange through the massive wall of windows, casting my elongated shadow over the golden shimmer of shrink-wrapped boxes and tempered-glass tanks. It was late, and we'd had a slow day, the teacher being only my fifth customer. Once that evening sun struck me, I felt sluggish, ready to slink home, microwave a salisbury steak, and then curl up for a nap.

I finally found the teacher giggling with Drew behind the turtle-care aisle. I ducked behind a stack of turtle food. I wanted to catch Drew in the act, find out what he was doing to steal my customers and get all those bonuses. Hidden behind bottles of Vitamin C–Enriched Turt-lets, I watched Drew dance in a little circle, swaying his hips, waving his arms, and slapping the leather elbow pads on the blazers he always wore to make himself look smarter than me, professorial. He halted, swung his arms out in a ta-da gesture. The teacher smiled with dimples and wide eyes. From Drew's right shirtsleeve, one of our adolescent boas poked its head, then slithered around his forearm, flicking its forked pink tongue at his palm.

I could've busted him right there, barged into his show, maybe used one of Rizzo's snake-handling poles to hook him by the nostril. But I wanted more than just grounds for a write-up. I wanted him gone, so he could make way for new blood.

The teacher dug through her purse for the five-dollar admittance to go to the basement, where we housed the Realm of the Reptiles exhibit. I hurried ahead of them, down the steps behind the sales counter, where I could hide among the reptiles—the perfect place to strike.

It wasn't much of an exhibit. A ramshackle version of the reptile house at the zoo. Ten- and twenty-gallon tanks cluttered the walls, crammed the hallway so that my arms brushed the glass, felt the skittering vibrations of lizards darting away to hide in their plastic shrubbery. I pushed through the hallway. The smell of frying cockroaches and regurgitated mouse scalp hung thick in the basement. I hated being down there, the darkness only broken by the massive fifty-tanker at the end of the hallway, glowing in the main room of the exhibit.

A secret I revealed to no one: I was terrified of the snakes.

I was an expert on all manner of reptilian products, but that didn't mean I wanted to drape a constrictor around my shoulders. Salmonella gathered for orgies on snake skin. Imminent sickness. Slow death. One touch and your skin would be infested.

Drew's boots clomped down the wooden stairs behind me, the teacher's giggles echoing over the hum of the UV lights. I squeezed into the glowing main room. In the main tank, Bertha, our mature black-tailed python, glared at me, her beady eyes sinister under the dark V on her brow. Ten feet of glossy, spotted skin uncoiled slowly. She made me shiver, my muscles contract, convulse. Like waking from a nightmare, where you don't remember why you're afraid but you feel it, the cold sweat, the rattling heart. That's caveman kind of fear, instinctual, evolutionary, necessary. I sucked in my gut, tightened my arms against my sides, and slid into the one good hiding place in the main room, right next to Bertha's tank.

Bertha was riled up, having sensed me. She wanted dinner, mice, rats, something exotic, like when Rizzo found baby raccoons in the attic and tossed the screeching infants in the tank. She engulfed those innocent babies, one after the other until they became bulges in Bertha's skin.

I felt Bertha's head smack her side of the glass, striking at the fake panorama of field grass pasted there. I winced each time she struck. My shirt had ridden up in my squirming, and the glass warmed my skin. I imagined her teeth digging into my soft flesh, her speared nose driving into my navel, glossy scales wrapping my intestines.

When Drew entered Bertha's room, he started dancing again, humming a slow, high-noted tune. He moved toward Bertha's tank. I heard the metal scratch of the latch lifted. From my vantage, I couldn't see what Drew was doing, but I guessed, swallowed dryly. And in a few seconds, Drew waltzed into the center of the dimly lit room with Bertha vining his shoulders. He offered his hand to the teacher. She took it, and the two of them danced with Bertha. Rizzo would have his head. We could go back to the old days when customers were won with expertise instead of good looks and flashy acts.

Drew leaned toward the teacher. Their lips touched, torsos pressed. The teacher hooked her leg around the back of Drew's knee. Bertha slithered off his shoulders, plunked onto the stained carpet. She'd done her part and wanted to hunt, seek out the escaped mice that often roamed the basement exhibit. Her tail swished the carpet.

Bertha must have smelled my sweat. She twisted toward me, her tongue snatching molecules of hot fear like a child catching snowflakes. I should have jumped out then, put Drew in a half nelson, muscled him to the floor, but I didn't. Bertha's eyes hypnotized me. Snake charming in reverse. I stared until her head disappeared into the shadow at my feet, then her body, then the tapping of her nose against the pleat of my slacks.

The teacher slammed Drew against a wall of chameleon cages, sucked his lower lip. Drew's fingers slipped beneath her shirt, climbed her belly, and fumbled with a breast. I felt myself growing. I didn't intend to watch—I was no pervert voyeur—but I needed to keep my mind off Bertha, all ten feet of her, which now wrapped around my leg, up my thigh, and was twisting higher. When I flexed my leg, her body squeezed. I tried to relax. She'd be to my midsection soon, squeeze tighter, strangling liver, then lungs. I wondered if she could fit my body inside her mouth if she really tried. I'd seen her jaws stretch, like when Rizzo finally found and trapped the raccoon mother. He'd tossed her in Bertha's cage just to see. And Bertha proved how much she could swallow—the burly mother raccoon was no match, just another lump under her skin. Surely I'd be more of a challenge. The weight I'd put on over the years, up to 250 pounds now, was for once a good thing, a defense.

Drew was lean, tall and skinny. The teacher had to reach her arms high over her head to wrestle the T-shirt off his body. He was hairy. All mammal. My chest and stomach only grew sparse sprigs of hair. I was mostly smooth, naturally so, sleekly so. If only I could talk to Bertha, I could convince her how much better of a meal Drew would make: easier to stretch into her jaws, better meat, worth the hairballs. I couldn't talk sense into Bertha, though. She was twisting through my legs, flexing over my erection. It had been so long since a woman had touched me. Bertha pulsed, pangs of serpentine pleasure I tried to ignore. Before us, the teacher grinded against Drew, the young college graduate, the handler of snakes, the tall and lean and desirable.

I couldn't take it, our paralleling embraces. I stomped onto Bertha's body. She tightened around my legs, strangling my erection until I thought it would pop. I ground my heel. We both strained, reacting to one another's struggle, fighting for our lives of lonely comfort, warm light and small cages.

The teacher went to pull up her shirt, but Drew stopped her. He led her away, probably out to his car or into Rizzo's office. Their footsteps scurried up the staircase. I grunted, leaned into my heel. Bertha slackened. I burst from the shadows, grabbed her head, and threw it to the floor. She zigzagged, banging into the walls, trying to scale them. I had to touch her, despite Rizzo's rule, a damn good one. I heaved her over my shoulders, struggling to drop her back into the tank. Under the bright lights, her body slumped, oozed blood from my footprint. There was no helping her, not that I wanted to.

Bertha had cursed me into having something in common with Drew. We'd both touched the snakes.

I headed upstairs and found Drew counting the till. He wasn't with the teacher, who had disappeared. I scanned for any last customers, locked the front doors.

"Did you see that chick?" Drew said.

"Where'd she go?"

"Bought three of our best heat lamps, a crate of turtle chow, and went on her way." He licked his fingers, shuffled through the bills.

"She's a teacher. What a looker, too. Wish we had about a hundred more customers like her."

"Did you give her a Realm of the Reptiles tour?" I pulled the counted till from Drew's hands, started recounting. It was my job.

"You know it." Drew punched my shoulder. I didn't return the smile spreading stupidly across his face. "In fact, she's bringing her whole class on Monday. Thirty kids."

"How the hell you gonna fit that many people downstairs at once?" I lost count of the till, the green bills blurring. I started over.

"That's where you come in. You can tour them around up here, teach them about reptiles and shit, while I give small group tours."

"You mean, while you screw around with their teacher?"

"What?"

I dropped the till, let it flutter in a messy pile on the counter. "While you touch the snakes?"

"I don't touch snakes." Drew looked up to the ceiling, scratched his chin. "I know Rizzo's rule."

"You don't know rules. You don't know reptiles. Just because you touch these snakes, you think you're king shit."

"Look, man," Drew put his hand on my shoulder, "I don't touch the snakes."

"Bullshit." I grabbed Drew by his blazer lapels, shook him.

"Wait. Wait." Drew squirmed, pushed his palms in my face. I released him, saw the frightened child in his eyes. He was just a kid playing games, didn't know any better.

He stumbled away from me. From each pocket of his blazer, he pulled a snake, another from his jeans. He held up his finger for me to wait while he dropped them into an empty tank. He had them everywhere, fearless of their coiling bodies.

"So, yeah, I touch the snakes. I touch them like you can't."

I wanted to correct him, lecture him about their bacteria-ridden skin. But I didn't get a chance. Drew cracked his knuckles, crouched into a wrestling stance, circled me. It was something like the dance I'd seen him do for the teacher, his shoulders bobbing, hips swaying. Rhythmic and natural.

"If violence is all you understand," Drew said, "so be it."

Drew pounced.

Our fight didn't last long. Drew was quick, swatted my ears, but I smothered him quickly, put him in a sleeper until he knelt on the tile floor. I didn't let go until he stopped squirming, until I lay on top of him, my body engulfing his. For a moment, I thought my sleeper hold had actually made him fall asleep. But he spoke.

"I'll give you one hundred. Two-thirds split from the teacher's class."

"What about Rizzo's cut?" I released Drew from the hold but remained on top of him.

"Rizzo will never know." He lay still under my belly, acquiesced to my weight. I was finally in control, like Drew with the snakes. "Fuck Rizzo's cut."

"Stop touching the snakes and we have a deal."

Drew didn't say anything. I didn't release him. Not yet. Not until I was sure he couldn't steal any more of my customers.

"I have to touch the snakes for the kids," Drew said to the floor. "Just this one last time, and then I'll never touch them again."

I leaned into Drew, felt his back tense, resisting my advantage, and then give in. I had him where I wanted him. This was better than catching Drew in the act, reporting him to Rizzo. His fingers would tremble when he passed the snakes in the weeks to come, but he couldn't touch them. He made a promise.

Work went smoothly the rest of the weekend. I raked in the sales, and Drew was helpless without his snakes. Every time a pretty girl or a group of kids walked in, he'd dig into his blazer pockets, then hang his head and slump back to the stockroom, where I hoped he was taking long, hard looks at Rizzo's sign. No one went downstairs, and Rizzo's was my domain once again, the showroom filled with shiny boxes, where expertise was king, instead of dark hallways cluttered with mystery, the touch of scaly skin and broken rules. That lasted until closing on Sunday, when Drew went to clean and feed the snakes downstairs.

"Something's wrong with Bertha." Drew's face had turned pale, his forehead creased.

We both made our way down, and I tried to look surprised when I saw Bertha's wound, the size of my footprint. It had blackened, and pus seeped from cracks in her skin, which had begun to prematurely shed. I didn't feel guilt. It was Drew's fault. He'd touched the snakes.

"The kids are coming tomorrow, man." Drew plucked at his leather elbow patches. "They can't see her like this."

"Did you touch Bertha?"

Drew's head drooped. He took a deep breath, tried to say something, but only let out a few choked sighs. When he lifted his head, I saw tears. He was playing the scared kid again. I didn't trust the tears. Last time, that scared kid pounced.

"Shit, man. You gotta help me." Drew put his hands on my shoulders. I could see, with his arms raised, the gaps in his fancy elbow patches. They were frayed, coming loose at the seams, like Bertha's flaking skin. I could have torn them off with one quick pull.

"Should we take her to the vet? You're the expert, man. What do we do?"

I was the expert, and Drew finally acknowledged that. But I didn't know anything about reptile emergencies. I knew how to thump a dead snake in the dumpster, and I knew how to feed and care for a live snake, but I didn't know the in-between, the near death. And I didn't want to save Bertha or Drew. It was time for me to think about myself, focus on my own survival. So I made a choice. We wouldn't touch Bertha. We'd wait until morning and see what happened.

Before we left that night, I smashed and sprinkled some vitamin-enriched snake pellets over a mouse and dropped it in Bertha's cage. I convinced Drew it would help. He looked hopeful when Bertha budged from her coil, her head following the mouse, tongue flicking. That was enough to get him through the night.

The next morning, Bertha was dead.

Drew came to work looking extra sophisticated, not just a blazer and jeans but a baby-blue button-up shirt, a striped satin tie, pleated slacks, and a new blazer. With how professional he looked, I thought he'd take Bertha's death in stride, philosophize coolly—just another dead snake in a world where so many snakes have passed before, where many more will be born—but he broke down. Not just tears. He whimpered, ran up the stairs, locked himself in the bathroom.

The teacher was coming in two hours, and she'd see what a fool Drew was, how he was all phony tricks, no expert of anything. That was the real reason he cried. It wasn't sympathy for Bertha; it was fear of his shed skin, of someone seeing the truth, the naked animal.

I put my ear against the bathroom door and heard Drew sniffle and pant. "We can still do it, Drew. It'll be great," I told him.

He opened the door, eyes red, lashes clumped. "You think so?"

"Sure. I'll be here to help. We'll make good money. The kids will love it."

"Thanks, man. I needed to hear that."

I never had kids, had no interest in pasting a Band-Aid over a skinned knee, a slab of frozen steak over a black eye. Drew couldn't lull me into parental bliss, as convincing as his crying act was. If he wanted to offer up the vulnerable child, I would devour it, grow stronger.

"But what about Bertha?" He pulled at his eyes with the backs of his fists. "Bertha's the main attraction."

"We'll say she's sleeping."

"No, man. We have to do better than that." His eyes were dry now, but he kept pulling at them with his sleeves. "You could control Bertha. You just have to touch her."

"She's dead, crawling with disease."

"You're scared. I get it." Drew's eyes widened, and each bloodshot vein seemed to slither. "It's okay if you are. Not everyone can touch the snakes like I do."

His eyes, those damn eyes. I stared through those squirmy

blood-filled capillaries. I could do anything Drew could—possess snake flesh and reptile knowledge simultaneously.

"I'm not afraid of touching the snakes," I said.

And Drew had a plan, a big one. He convinced me to climb into the cupboard under Bertha's fifty-tanker, convinced me with the challenge of flesh and fear. And there I was, pretzeled into a tiny box.

The cupboard was cramped and hot from Bertha's heat lamp. I bowed my head so low that my ear pressed against my stomach. In one ear, I heard my breakfast churning. In the other, the children upstairs tapped across the floor, hollering, probably looking at all our complicated products in wonder, with no one but Drew to fumble over false explanations. It was too bad they'd miss out on that education, but Drew said the show came first, said the snakes were most important, interest before intellect.

They'd be headed down to explore the Realm of the Reptiles soon. I lifted my hand through the hole Drew and I had cut into the glass bottom of Bertha's cage. I watched Bertha's slumped carcass through another smaller hole we'd cut so I could see what I was doing. But I didn't want to see Bertha. She made my muscles twitch. Even in death, she scared me.

My fingers found her skin. It was hot but lifeless, so different from a few days ago when I'd thrown her from my body, when each scale pulsed. I wished I'd worn gloves, but Drew had laughed when I suggested them.

I groped until I found the slit Drew had made, the half-moon he'd sliced through her underbelly with a box cutter. He'd dug out a fistful of Bertha innards, just enough so I could fit my hand inside. He'd gutted her so easily, even after all those tears, all his affection for the snakes. He'd torn away pink shreds of Bertha. And now it was my turn to be even colder than Drew, better than Drew. I fingered the opening and pushed my hand forward. If Drew could do it, I could. Her flesh squished against my knuckles. Through the peephole, I saw the upraised veins in my wrist, where they ended, where the snake became my hand.

I lowered my wrist, and then there was only Bertha. Drew had sliced and gutted only a few inches from her head, had cut the hole in the glass with enough clearance so I had a decent range of motion. When I moved my hand, Bertha slithered, alive again. Bertha and me. We longed for Drew, for him to challenge us, to set us in motion.

Children's shrieks and gasps echoed off the glass walls of the Realm of the Reptiles. I still couldn't see them, my vision confined to the tiny peephole showing only dead Bertha and darkness beyond her bright cage. But then a face appeared, wide eyes, a mussed towhead, mouth gaping. Then more, a dozen children silhouetted by the shadows, all staring down at Bertha, at me. My fist inside Bertha's skin convulsed. Whatever way I moved Bertha felt phony. I didn't understand a snake's movement, and the children looked bored, their mouths closing, eyes flitting away to see the genuine life the Realm of the Reptiles had to offer. I was losing them.

Drew appeared before the tunneled vision of my peephole. Rizzo's snakes draped his arms, his neck, crawling and arching their heads, flicking their tongues. The children turned toward him, faces glowing with excitement again. They danced around him, and I thought of St. Patrick driving the snakes into the sea, tricking the last old serpent. Drew neared my cage, the young teacher gripping his shoulder, the children shepherded by him and his snakes. They peered into my tank again, examined the intricacies of my scaled body, my cloudy eyes now aimed at Drew, waiting.

He clicked the latch at the top of the tank. The metal vibrated through the glass, into Bertha, into me. He was coming to make us alive and real. He lowered one hand into the tank, and I stared at it, hungry for inspiration. His palms were smooth and glowing under the lights. I could almost feel their warmth, the desire to crawl into them, slide up his arm, wrap around the leather elbow patches. He waved his hand, and I followed. I used my own eyes at first, but as I began to sway, I felt Bertha, sensed those tiny black beads. He swirled his hand, and I followed again, twisting, circles, dizzying. My cramped, overweight body below disappeared. No arms, no legs. I became sleek and strong.

Then Drew made a fist. I froze. Our eyes trained on each other, locked, bonded. The fist poofed into wiggling fingers, and I felt myself again, my neck cramping, my back aching, my hand sweating inside Bertha's hot guts.

The children clapped, cheered. The teacher pecked Drew secretly on the cheek. He looked satisfied, his lips curling slightly at the edges. Not saved, not relieved, but satisfied. He was not a child to save or devour. Here were children, eyes big and white and empty. A python like Bertha could birth one hundred children in one pop. This crowd would mean nothing to her. But they meant everything to me, this audience witnessing my hand becoming serpent.

And he was not the professor in his blazer and tie. Here was a teacher, at his side, just as charmed by him as the children were. Drew was something else, something I'd never known, something that had hypnotized me to swirl and swoop and turn into a human pretzel.

So what was I?

I had touched the snake, violated Rizzo's sacred commandment. But it wasn't that simple. I had been Bertha, and I was, as she had been, one of Drew's reptilian passengers, his cold-blooded followers looking for warmth, for the light.

The children and the teacher scattered away from the cage. Drew remained, his face illuminated in a backdrop of darkness. I tried to wriggle free from Bertha's skin grown tight around my wrist. I shook her dead weight. Drew backed away, into the shroud of shadows. Alone, I struggled, finally shed her. I shoved Bertha's slumped body aside and gazed through the peephole at my own hand, coated in coagulated snake blood, but, yes, my hand. I raised it higher, flailed inside the glass, hoping someone would see my bright hand, the possessor of knowledge, tricked and trapped in this tiny box, but no one saw.

THE FIRE CHASERS

AT HOME RANDALL COULD QUIETLY CELEBRATE HIS PROMO-
tion to head safety supervisor at the refinery. He pulled a cigar
and book of matches from his pocket, lifted his knuckles to his
nose, and smelled the oil soaked into his fingers. The match head
scraped across the strike strip and fizzled white. He waved his fingers
through the tiny flame, and the oil in his skin did not ignite, would
not burn and turn to ash, as his job would not burn, despite the
refinery announcing shutdown, despite the layoffs and thinning
number of men who entered the cyclone fence at punch in. He lit
his cigar. He stayed still while the big lilac bush bent toward him
in the summer breeze, the small petals teasing the burning ember
in his mouth. It was a good thing to stand still and let the world
sway around him, especially after a long shift climbing tanks and
towers, tugging the men's lanyards, checking for gloves, making
sure they weren't smoking.

He puffed hard, made the cherry glow bright orange under a
pinecone of gray ash. His little fire at home. At work everything
could burn. All the petroleum would burn eventually. From his
house, he could see the whip of flame spouting from the burn-off
tower at the refinery, waving to him, saying, Goodbye. See you
tomorrow. You'll be back.

His twelve-year-old son, Jackson, scraped a jackknife through the bark of their maple tree. The boy's long hair hid his face, so Randall couldn't tell if he was scraping with anger or boredom or what. Maybe Jackson was carving a heart, his initials over some young girl's. Maybe Jackson's initials grooved dark and jagged above some boy's.

Sirens blared down the street, and Jackson's skinny arms froze. His knife dropped to the dirt. Randall's house squatted only a few blocks from the station, and he'd grown used to the trucks' constant whines that summer. It sounded like two trucks, maybe three. A good-sized fire. Three trucks were plenty for the few thousand homes in their small Michigan town. Homes built around the refinery, Dow Chemical, Alma Bolt, the sugar beet factory. Randall's refinery had its own trucks, better, newer, had its own hoses and gallons of foam and shiny red extinguishers placed every few yards along the catwalks, had its own coal-filter respirators and heavy yellow jackets hung like deflated men in the break-room closet.

The fire truck lights sparked red through the fat plumage of his maple tree. Randall's chest was bare, but he didn't have time to go inside and get a T-shirt. He bit into the butt of his cigar and jogged to his van. He turned the key twice before the engine gurgled to life. Outside the passenger's window, his son stared. He could see Jackson's face now, pale with a slightly sunken chin, small nose, all framed with that long dirty-blond hair.

Randall leaned over the seat and cranked down the window. "If you wanna see this fire, you better get moving."

Jackson lowered his head and trudged toward the van. Randall drummed the steering wheel with his fingertips as the trucks surged down their road. Finally the passenger door creaked open, and Jackson climbed onto the seat.

Randall caught up to the trucks after a few blocks. He matched their speed, slicing through red-light intersections. He smiled over at Jackson, who was looking out the window instead of watching the lights, the chrome fenders, the beast of a truck ahead of them.

"You're going to miss all the best stuff." Randall elbowed his son.

His boy turned toward the fire trucks but didn't smile back, didn't look his father in the eye. Randall had only had one kid with Celia. Jackson cost enough, they'd both agreed years ago. And Randall had worried about every outlet in the house, every stair step, every sharp corner. He hadn't wanted to go through that terror again. But now he thought about another son, or a daughter. His promotion confirmed he could protect them, even in the dry summers like this one, where roofs spurted flames almost every night. But he worried about Jackson, how to save him from the whitewashes and swirlies and black eyes he got at school. He imagined outfitting him in a suit of muscles and calluses, like slipping a wool safety jacket onto the men at work.

"How fast do you think they can go?" Jackson pointed ahead of them. His fingernails were painted black. A mood ring strangled the knuckle of his middle finger. A row of wire twist ties adorned his thumb.

"What's this faggy shit about?" Randall said, grabbing Jackson's broomstick wrist.

"I don't know."

"You go to the beauty salon to get that done?"

Jackson's sunken chin sucked tight against his collarbone, and Randall wished he hadn't said anything. Maybe doing nothing was better. Jackson would survive school, would fuck girls and tell his dad about it over beers someday. Randall just had to wait.

He followed the trucks onto Amber Street and saw the smoke rolling east over moss-scabbed shingles. So close to his neighborhood, like the last five fires. The trucks groaned to a stop in front of the Leylands' house.

Randall parked, and before getting out he grabbed his name tag from the cup holder. Etched into the polished metal, tall letters spelled his title at work. He slid the name tag into his pocket and then worked his way toward a crowd already gathered on the sidewalk around the Leylands' new add-on. Jackson scurried in the opposite direction, across the street to the sidewalk, where it was safe, where three old ladies were gabbing.

The Leylands' house was close to theirs but closer to the golf course, where Randall had played with borrowed clubs a few times. Mr. Leyland had a membership, until he was laid off from his position as senior quality inspector at Playbuoy Pontoons last month. The Leylands lived on the border, a line down Decatur Avenue that separated new aluminum siding from sun-blistered pine, lawns patched yellow from thick green sod. Jackson took his place on the brittle yellow side while Randall joined the crowd around the Leylands' wilting sod.

The fire crawled up the aluminum siding. The metal already drooped, singed black. The flames swung like hair in the wind, auburn hair, shocks of bright yellow, a flash of blue springing when the gusts blew.

"That's the goddamned baby's room," somebody in the crowd said. "Just built that add-on for her last year. I bet she's still in there." The speaker had a brown mustache, ropey arms, wore a stained yellow tank top. He was hard to recognize without his coveralls, away from the stacks, but the tattoo of Saint Florian's Roman skirt and muscular thighs gave Vance away. Florian's gold armor was hidden under Vance's yellowed bandages. The refinery had fired him three weeks ago, just after Randall had caught him smoking on the catwalks. Vance had been a good worker, but good work meant nothing without safety.

"I think I hear it crying," someone else said.

"I'm going in if that baby's not out in the next thirty seconds," Vance said. "The rest of you civilians should step away."

"These boys can handle it," Randall said. He stepped in front of the crowd, spread his arms wide, and planted them over the Leylands' fence. "It'll be safe."

"Shit, Randall," Vance said, brushing up his mustache, "I'm a full-on substitute firefighter now. It's my responsibility to watch out for the public."

"The public's fine." Randall reached into his pocket, thumbed the grooved letters of his name tag. The grooves felt shallow, the letters numb to his callused thumb.

"Twenty seconds, and I'm going in." Vance crossed his arms, flexed the forearm that wielded Florian's fancy skirt.

Two firemen clomped through the front door. Randall squinted at the fire knocking at the second-story window, where a baby may or may not have been. He imagined the window shattering, Mrs. Leyland clutching a blanketed bundle of screeching. She'd yell to the crowd, toss her baby through the flames as if it were a bouquet. Vance would dive too early, and Randall would catch it. No one else, because he was calm, because fire didn't scare him. Jackson would lift his sunken chin and nod to his father.

The wind blew hard, and the fire surged toward the crowd. Someone screamed. Randall felt the heat against his chest. He gripped the fence harder, facing down the orange shoulder that jutted toward him. The hair on his knuckles tightened, curled, cowering into a sizzle.

Randall didn't move until a fireman pushed his chest. "All the way back," the fireman shouted to the crowd. "See that kid on the other side of the street." He shot a gloved finger at Jackson. "He's the only one with any sense."

"You heard the man." Vance slapped the fireman's back, remained at the fence while the crowd wandered across the street, all walking backward, staring at the blaze. Randall tailed the crowd, watching them, their eyes reflecting fire, the black Os of their mouths. He outstretched his arms and waved his fingers, corralling the slow-moving crowd as Vance had neglected to do. By the time he got to Jackson, the hydrant hose had rushed to life. The fire fizzled quickly under the water and made the Leylands' sidewalk glisten. The hydrant runoff puddled halfway across the road, but it wasn't enough to reach the sunbaked grass on their side.

Out the front door came Mr. Leyland, one of the firemen fingering his upper back. Then came Mrs. Leyland, holding the baby. It was fat and pink and not wrapped in blankets as he'd imagined. It didn't cry. The hose pounded the last whips of fire, and the crowd cheered.

One of the firemen tossed Vance a Polaroid camera. The flash lit up the smoke-stained siding. Vance fired off a dozen shots, slipping each one into his back pocket. Then he turned his back to the house, aimed the camera at the crowd, and took one shot.

Randall watched Vance flick the last picture he'd taken. Around Randall, men stood shirtless, dirty nails and mussed hair, frayed jean shorts. One of them held a can of beer. Randall wished he had somewhere to pin his tag and could almost feel the sting from the hole he'd pierce through his chest.

Randall and his boy pulled into the driveway, and he noted that their brittle yellow lawn needed watering. He gripped his doorknob, which needed the right jiggle to open, which would cost precious seconds in an emergency. He worked the knob and opened the door for his son but didn't follow him.

The air was calm, and away from his home the burn-off tower's flame shot straight up. The waving hand had changed into one giant orange finger pointing up. But there was nothing higher to point to in Alma than this burning finger, and the fire wouldn't stop burning, wouldn't be put out by Alma firemen with their hydrants and Vance's Polaroids, wouldn't stop until Randall supervised shutdown.

Randall slipped through his front door. In the kitchen, Celia poured a glass of lemonade for Jackson. His bony fingers gripped the glass, the black fingernails looking like dead holes against his pale skin. Jackson gulped down the glass, set it on the counter, and Celia poured again.

"Another fire?" Celia ran her fingers through the boy's hair as he sipped the next glass. Her fingernails were short and unpainted.

"Everyone's okay. They saved a baby."

He stared at his boy's black nails until Jackson clunked the glass on the counter and wormed out of the room.

"The fires are all over, Randy," Celia rinsed the glass, ran a dingy rag over the rim. "This whole town is going up."

"We're safe." Randall reached above her and pressed their smoke detector. The alarm didn't sound.

"This town just needs some damn rain. The town gets crazy when it's just hot and dry all the time."

"I can't make it rain." Randall opened the junk drawer to search for a battery.

"I didn't ask you to." She raised a cigarette to her lips. "No jobs, no rain, nothing anyone can do about it."

But Randall had a job, a promotion even, and it would last until the refinery tower's flame snuffed out. Randall rummaged through the drawer but couldn't find a battery. Instead, he pulled out a book of matches and tore one off for his wife.

Celia ignored him and cupped her hands over her lighter. "What'd Jackie think of the fire?"

Randall wished his wife would use their boy's legal name, Jackson, a solid name. Jackie was paper-thin, crumpled under the tongue. "What the fuck is with his nails? Is that your paint?"

"I found a quart of paint in his room. It's your paint. The stuff you used on the shutters. You ever see my nails black?"

He remembered her nails being orange last week when he took her out to Pizza Sam's to celebrate rumors of his promotion, rumors he'd joked about with the men on the stacks. Safety supervisor wasn't work, but a desk and a clipboard and probably a skirt, the men had said.

"What's wrong with him?"

"Phases, baby." She passed her cigarette to Randall. A pink smudge of lipstick ringed the filter. He waved it away. "You gotta be able to laugh about this stuff."

"I just wish he'd bring home a girl or something. Just so I wouldn't have to worry."

"Jesus, he's twelve. I'll take black nails over some knocked-up teenager."

Randall finally discovered some batteries at the back of the drawer. He opened the detector and found the batteries missing. He popped in the new ones.

"I found a job in the paper I might apply to," Celia said.

"We have lots of time still. You don't need a job."

"Can't pass up an opportunity. We might need the only job in town after the refinery closes." She dropped her cigarette butt into the disposal.

"We got another year at least, probably more. And then there's the demo. I'll have plenty to do. I'll be the very last one to go." She flipped the switch for the disposal. The blades whirred against the cotton filter, kicked smoke out of the sink. He smelled burnt tobacco and cotton. It smelled like when Vance had caught fire smoking, when Randall had known exactly what to do. The smoke detector's alarm blared. Celia opened the window over the sink. The alarm silenced, but Randall's ears kept ringing.

Randall had too much time on the weekends now. The refinery had cut Saturdays indefinitely. He thumbed his old baseball glove in the garage, wondered if it would still fit. He unzipped his hunting rifle, ran his fingers down the stock, zipped the bag back up. He kicked at a pile of two-by-fours, pulled his tool belt from a rusty nail. It smelled like sweat and leather and grease. Like work, real work. But behind that smell, Randall's hands smelled like oranges. The commercial soap in his new office now overpowered the petroleum. Celia used to push him away, when he first started working the stacks. She'd push him into the shower and laugh, threaten jamming soap in his mouth to kill the fire on his breath. But she got used to the smell.

Everyone in Alma got used to the smell of the refinery, of petroleum. But not Randall. He was ever vigilant. Someone had to be. That was Vance's problem. The petroleum had become a part of him, a smell as familiar as his own sweat. Vance had been leaning over the catwalk, an unlit cigarette dangling from his lips. Randall had only started down the catwalk when Vance spun the flint on his lighter. His hands flashed, fingertips stretching in orange. Frozen, Vance had stared at his flaming fingers, as if trying to decipher refinery-stack schematics. Randall clanged across the catwalk. No dirt to smother Vance's body with, Randall tackled him, hugged him against his coveralls. He held him there, two men clutching at each other. A group below hollered, "Get a room." Vance had fought against Randall's grip until he finally slammed Vance's head against the metal grates. The refinery was happy to have any excuse to fire him, and Vance was gone the next day, Randall promoted. Since that day, Randall carried no tool belt, never lingered on the stacks among the men for longer than it took to check their safety equipment.

Randall hung the tool belt back on the wall. Outside the dusty panes on the garage side door, Jackson was plucking crab apples. The boy squished the berries and pulled the pulp through his hair.

Randall lifted his gas can from behind the mower. Jackson had mowed earlier, even though there was nothing to cut, the lawn yellow and dead. Randall cracked the side door.

"What the hell are you doing, Jackson?"

The boy dropped a handful of crab apples. "Nothing." They skittered across the patio concrete. "I don't know."

Jackson's easy answer. A boy's answer. Randall's job required complete knowledge of where each thin white ladder connected to every catwalk at the refinery, how every catwalk led to stairs, to ground, to the front gate, where each man would eventually exit forever. He stepped onto the patio and felt a berry burst under his sandal.

"Why are you putting that shit in your hair?"

"An experiment, I guess." Jackson dragged his foot over a pile of crab apples. "It's stupid."

"Don't eat those."

"I'm not dumb," Jackson said, scraping his sneaker against the concrete, curling the berry flesh into tiny twisted fingers.

"I want to show you something." Randall held the side door for Jackson, who passed under his arm. He could smell the bitter fruit in his boy's hair.

Randall set the gas can in front of them, squatted, unscrewed the top. A stream of invisible waves floated out the spout, and he looked up at his boy through water, through molten glass, there waiting to learn something with crab apple experiments crushed into his long hair.

"If you're mowing, you should know how to put out a gas fire."
He tipped the can, let a stream puddle on the floor. He hovered over the puddle, but it didn't burn his eyes or sting his nose. He was still immune to petroleum. His boy sniffled, wiped his nose, smearing a burgundy stain across his upper lip.

Randall dropped a match onto the puddle, and a rush of blue waved over it. Deep-orange tails spiked and split. Randall watched his boy, watched the fire. He had an urge to dump more gas, maybe toss in his old glove or his tool belt. He wanted Jackson to move close enough to feel the heat on his ankles. But his boy stayed at a safe distance.

The fire died, and only a black smudge remained on the garage floor.

"So you just let it burn out?" Jackson asked.

Randall kicked at the smudged floor until he'd made a hole of lighter gray around the black. A missing spot. Even what remained after the fire could be erased.

"No," Randall said. "You use dirt."

The next one happened that Sunday, and it smelled like a bonfire. Randall had felt it tingling in his fingers as soon as he woke up, knew it would happen soon. And then he smelled it from inside the house, where Celia smoked below an empty smoke detector. Her nostrils flared as she examined her cigarette. He ran to the bedroom, pulled on a pair of jeans, and buttoned up his supervisor shirt. He pinned his metal name tag to the breast pocket.

He strode down the hallway but stopped at Jackson's closed door. He knocked, and when the boy didn't answer, he cracked the door and watched his son through a slice. Inside, Jackson sat cross-legged on his bed with a red pincushion beside his thigh. He wore a shirt with pearl buttons and gray flowers. He was bothering one of his fingers with a pin and hid his hand once he saw Randall.

"We got another fire, Jackson. You coming?"

"I don't know." Jackson trained his eyes on his bare toes, his hand still behind his back.

"What's to know? You're coming, or you're not."

The fire trucks still hadn't started their whine. If he hurried, he could beat them.

"I'm kind of busy with this." The boy removed the hand from his back. Two needles stuck through the skin on each fingertip. They formed ten crosses on his left hand.

A grunt slipped from Randall's chest. Jackson lowered his head. Maybe it was time the boy heard a grunt like this. He'd hear it from others. Needles and berries and painted fingernails. It was a combination that added up to nothing useful.

"I'd come," Jackson said, "but I have to pull out my crosses." He lifted his left hand to Randall. "It might hurt."

"Let me see." Randall gripped the boy's wrist, squinted at the needles. They'd raised pale humps of crisscrossing skin, something like a star. Not a drop of blood though. "They're just through your calluses. You can't feel anything there."

Randall pinched a needle head and pulled. Jackson hissed through his front teeth, and he told the boy to look away for the next one. When he pulled again, Jackson didn't react, couldn't even tell, and Randall smiled at his work. There was still no clamor from the fire station, but the smoke was heavier now. Somewhere a fire. Perhaps another baby surrounded by smoke or a mother or a father who didn't know what to do. At the thumb, Randall pulled too hard, and the boy's wrist jerked. A dot of red welled from his skin. Randall wiped it with his shirtsleeve, and his boy's blood left a black stain.

"Sorry, Jackson," he said.

"It's okay." Jackson smiled. "I didn't even really feel it."

They followed the wind-sliced puffs of smoke on foot. Still no sound from the station. Randall could have reported the fire, but the city should've known the difference between the burning leaves that sputtered and spewed gray from the black clouds of treated lumber.

Jackson chewed his fingertips as they walked down Amber. Randall tried to ignore his boy's clicking teeth. He unpinned his name tag and polished it with the inside of his sleeve. They turned south, and the smoke grew, veiling the burn-off tower on the horizon. Randall wanted to run, but Jackson only plodded along. The whole town seemed slow. A fire burned close, but no sirens, no hydrant rush, no screaming women or babies. Just tree leaves shuddering and the tick of Jackson's teeth against his skin.

When they turned down Mill, they found the fire. A small shed spit flames into the air outside Vance's house. Randall wondered if that was why the fire station hadn't sprung to life, if being a substitute fireman offered the privacy of handling your own fire.

Vance leaned against the faded siding of his house, studying the fire as it crept across his yellow grass. He carried no extinguisher, wore no heavy jacket or wader boots. Vance's bare torso gleamed with sweat all the way to his bandaged arm. His hair was matted on one side, as if he'd been napping.

Randall straightened his name tag. "Need some help?"

"I have a shovel, but it's in the shed," he nodded to the door, "and that's kind of fucked now."

"Could spread to the house."

"It's under control."

Vance stepped closer to the fire between them. Randall readied himself for the flames to spring up Vance's arms, and then he'd wrestle this man, naked to the waist, into the dirt in front of his son. They'd both be filthy, soot covered, his name tag and button-up shirt unrecognizable. And then the fire would spread to Vance's house, down the street, dancing across rooftops, northbound.

Jackson stepped away from his father, toward the fire, and Randall wanted to reach for his boy. He didn't know if he could wrestle two bodies to the ground, if he was strong enough to clunk Jackson's head against the earth until he submitted.

Jackson reached Vance and dug his hands into the dirt, worked an arcing trough around the fire. Randall felt hot in his shirt. He rolled up his sleeves. Down the street, no crowd approached to gawk, so he watched his son, watched as Vance slowly circled around his house and returned carrying a two-by-four, which he plunged into the dirt. He dug alongside Jackson, thrusting the board with his good hand

and steadying it with his fist full of bandages. As Vance worked, the bandages slipped up his arm, past the tattoo of Saint Florian's fancy skirt, exposing the golden breastplate. Randall sweated under his shirt. It was just the heat of the day. It was just the weight of his uniform. It was just the distance of his son, the length of Vance's yard, the fire that could leap across the brittle grass.

After a half hour, Vance and Jackson had circled the shed with a dirt trough. The walls of the shed collapsed and huffed a swarm of sparks at Jackson, but he didn't run, didn't scream, kept working the dirt, until the shed smoldered into a pile of black ash. Vance dropped his two-by-four and reached his hand out to Jackson. They shook, both their hands thick with dirt and sweat.

"Shame about your shed," Randall said, and wished he had something better to say, something about bandages and catwalks and how no one would be walking them soon.

"Nothing we could do." Vance scratched his chin, left fingerprints of dirt. "Thanks for lending me a helper."

"How'd it start?"

"This whole town's burning up," Vance pulled his dirty bandage back down over Saint Florian's armor. "Not much anyone can do but sign insurance checks."

Jackson returned to his father's side, and when Randall looked down at his boy's hands, the little white stars of raised skin were covered by a layer of dirt. They were still there, though. It would only take a little water, a little scrubbing, and his boy's stars would return.

On their way home, the skies turned gray for the first time in weeks. They walked past yards spitting flames. The citizens of Alma were dumping gas and turpentine and lighter fluid onto piles of old brush, dragging discarded lumber through their brittle grass to the flames, racing to beat the rain. At one house, a family circled their fire, tossed broken toys onto their burn pile. Three children danced and laughed as a red tricycle shriveled and spewed black smoke.

The smells of sweat and petroleum twisted through the cool breeze. Salt and petroleum. It was a bad mix. Not much you could do with the two together. Bury it. Bury contamination and hope no one finds out. And they wouldn't until demo, until the stacks and tanks were felled, until they tilled up the earth and found a useless, dangerous patch of dirt.

Randall wanted to run, get home, lock the doors, and phone the police to report all the illegal fires that could sprint across the dry earth at any moment, collide at his front door and shoot into the air as tall as the burn-off tower. But Jackson slowed him, stopping every few yards to pick up a stray stick or wilting dandelion and weave it into his hair. His hands twitched with the urge to slap all the twigs out of Jackson's hair. The heat in his cheeks dripped under his work shirt, collected around the pin of his name tag. He imagined the metal around his name, his title, turning orange, the engraved letters melting away into an illegible script. How would others read that he was the one watching over their safety? Soon enough, no one would know, when the refinery was just a plot of dirt caged by cyclone fences.

Jackson dipped to slip another dandelion behind his ear. Randall felt the townspeople staring through their fires at his boy, calling him queer under the crackles of brush. He wondered if Vance would tell people how Jackson had saved his house, Randall his life, or if the only story told would be of the two men who'd violently embraced on the refinery catwalks.

Randall jogged away from his boy toward a pair of men drinking cans of Pabst in front of a burning pile of siding that was already spreading through the grass to their sandaled toes. The men looked familiar, might have worked at the refinery once. He bent down, plucked a dandelion from their yard, and slipped it underneath his name tag.

The men laughed. The heat under his shirt cooled. He felt the breeze blowing harder, from the west, where the heavy gray clouds grew to drown the yellow grass of his neighborhood and sizzle the remains of Vance's smoldering shed, of all the burning junk of Alma. With the clouds, the fires would end. His son would be safe in a town where everything could no longer burn.

SUBDIVISION ACCIDENTS

THE STONEMASONS' LEFT ARMS TURNED GREEN IN THE MORN-ing, black by lunch, and then fell off like chewed cherry stems near quitting time. I watched through the window and hugged my cutting pot, nearly dropped my paintbrush, when all those blackened twists dropped from the scaffold, rolled onto the lush sod. The stonemasons cut out early, went home to their wives and sons. No one went to Jiffy Quick Care to see Doc Robby.

But I went. Doc Robby examined my arm, told me I had a fine shoulder. I had him examine my forearm, my bicep, squeeze each of the calluses on my fingers. Everything checked out A-okay. He said stethoscopes weren't for arms, but he listened. Sounds like an arm, he told me. But I had to be sure. If something happened to me, where would my family be?

The next day, the stonemasons returned with one giant brown wing sprouting from each of their left shoulders where their arms had died. Each flapped his one gigantic wing and gripped a trowel in the other arm. They flew around the subdivisions, bouncing off the freshly shingled roofs, zigzagging from one cul-de-sac to the next. Even though they flew mostly in drunken circles, they didn't need ladders for the facades anymore. They were faster, better, and the new wings smelled clean like turpentine.

"How do you like that," I said to Martha, my wife, who was also the cleaning lady. But she'd already slipped upstairs to spritz blue stuff at the new windows. Betsy, her daughter, heard me. She was scrubbing the brand-new downstairs toilet. The contractors weren't supposed to use the new toilets, but we did. Beat the Port-a-Johns, beat staring into that cave of chemicals filled with withered and castoff stonemason arms.

"I don't like it much at all," Betsy said, "but this is how we pay rent."

"I meant the stonemasons, hon," I said to no one, because the new toilets were clean and Betsy had joined her mother upstairs. I stood in the spotless living room, surrounded by my immaculate white walls, alone with my two good arms.

Us painters are always the last ones to leave a new house. There's always touch-up to do, even after the cleaning. Everybody mucks up my work. Hell, even Martha's and Betsy's brooms leave black scuffs against the baseboards, and I have to paint it all nice and white and shiny again. With my caulk and spackle and paint, I fix every flaw, cover every sign that anyone worked here.

The trim carpenters followed the stonemasons. It started with Fred buzzing off his index finger with the circular. Made a damn mess for Martha and Betsy. They went through three paper-towel rolls. We looked all over for Fred's finger, but he eventually told us to forget it. Not worth the trouble. I wanted to argue and peeked inside my cutting pot, because you never know. Just paint, though. Just white. Like every house in the subdivisions.

I told Fred to go see Doc Robby at Jiffy Quick Care. He grunted, curled his lips, said maybe he'd take the rest of the day off. And then his helper, Stanley "High Standards" Thompson, interrupted our conversation by zipping off his index finger with the same circular. Three more paper rolls. No sight of fingers. Not even in my cutting pot.

Turned out, all three of the trim-carpenter crews at the subdivisions had the same issue that day. All drove home at two o'clock, shooting past Jiffy Quick Care, crimson-stained paper towels wadded over their fists.

I made it to Jiffy Quick Care when I wrapped up around seven. I parked right next to Doc Robby's Taurus, nodded at his license plate, which read INAJIFF. This time, I had him check my legs, my toes, especially the toenail that'd been split for two years, ever since I kicked a full five-gallon bucket when I found out Betsy had started dating that roofer. Nothing new there. I dropped my pants, asked him if that was a hernia. He apologized for cold hands. "Anything you notice, Doc?" I asked. "Anything at all." He checked some boxes on my chart, pushed some trial Ameliorex pain pills with a knowing smile. On my way out, I tossed them to a fellow wearing a Hooter's apron in the waiting room.

Next day, the trim carpenters showed up on-site wielding scabbed stumps. The missing fingers showed up, too. They'd worked through the whole night and now worked alongside their previous owners. They were emancipated but cheap labor, accepted a fraction of minimum wage relative to their physical size. Those fingers did fine work and proved more useful detached and freethinking.

I was brushing some trim, watching a group of index fingers ahead of me feel out the baseboards for the shiners that used to piss me off when I had to set them. Three indexies lugged a hammer and thumped a nail head home. I called to Betsy, "Aren't those indexies a nice lot?"

But Betsy wasn't there. I hadn't seen her all day. She was growing up quick from the freckled seven-year-old with mismatched socks I met when Martha and I started working together. Betsy used to conduct weddings for Martha's spray bottles—now presenting Mr. and Mrs. Windex-Bleach. She was a young lady now, wielding spray bottles that couldn't exchange vows. Could have been twenty-five with her own cleaning crew and an armful of baby the next time I blinked my eyes.

Martha said, "I wish some of you boys would take your shoes off."

I turned from my window trim to see Martha on her hands and knees scrubbing at a sooty boot print in the berber. Must have been from the heating-and-cooling guys, who were bursting into flames every ten minutes.

"Do you think it hurts?" I said to Martha's back. "I never see blisters or boils or burnt flesh or boo-boos of any form. But it's gotta hurt."

"The floors are filthy."

"I suppose there's that."

"Everyone makes a mess." Martha sprayed more stain remover on the berber. It foamed bright like spilled white paint.

"I don't make a mess." I lifted up my feet to show her the paper booties I'd graciously slipped over my sneakers. Martha didn't look.

"The carpet guys are pretty clean, too."

"Well, it's their carpet." Martha whistled when she wiped the foam away and the boot print was gone. "They still put their hands all over the windows, piss all over the toilet seat."

"And don't forget what they do to my walls."

Martha swish-swished her broom up the stairway. I could have followed her, and perhaps I should have because it was our anniversary, married twelve years. I hoped she'd find the love letter on the wall in the master bedroom. But I wrote it with the touch-up paint, and it blended perfectly into the wall. At least the white walls would make her think of me.

I thought about the carpet guys. We were the same men we'd always been, nothing new, just doing our jobs and then trying to forget about them once we got home and watched baseball or played solitaire or stitched a new teal square into our quilts.

Across the road, through the big bay window, I saw Hank the head carpet layer kick through a front door, a giant roll of padding slung over his shoulder. I headed to the house across the street and followed his banging through the hallway, tracked his path of gouges and scrapes on my walls. He looked the same as always. Hank was just Hank, until another Hank walked through the door, a slightly smaller Hank with an armload of tack strip. More Hanks knocked through the entryway. Each one a little smaller. They were identical, wore the same stonewashed jeans with smaller and smaller holes in the knees. The same brown mustache covered their lips, the same uneven sideburns. Just smaller. Altogether, there were twelve, the tallest one Hank's original size, the shortest standing up to midshin. They scuffed my walls at every height.

"Did you get hurt?" I asked a Hank who stood as tall as my waist. "Tell me how it happened."

"Ask the boss." The midsized Hank nodded under the weight of his half-sized padding roll.

"Just point to where it hurts," I told full-sized Hank. "Did you see a doc?"

But it turned out who I thought was full-sized Hank was 91.66667 percent–sized Hank, and he pointed an elbow to another Hank, who sipped a thermos full of coffee in the corner.

Full-sized Hank said, "Who needs a doc? You need to stop worrying about me and us and our treacherous run-in with carpet glue and start worrying about touching up these walls. They're a mess."

Full-sized Hank took a long sip. So long I thought he'd drown. He finally lowered his thermos and breathed. He folded his arms and smiled at all the smaller-sized Hanks hard at work, bolting the tack strips to the subfloor, leaning over less than Hank used to have to lean. His back problems would be no more.

I went to lunch, to Ivan's Bread and Brew, down the street from the subdivisions where we all worked. The store squatted like a scab against a background of new white houses. I could see every nail in the sun-faded brown clapboard. Big nail heads pounded by healthy contractors who'd made sure their work would last and didn't care how it looked. I wondered if anyone who lived in the A-frame ranches and split-levels would go to Ivan's after we finished construction and disappeared. But where were we going? There was a world of soybean fields and forests and clapboard to tear up and cover with white walls and sod.

I ordered my usual turkey and cream cheese bagel sandwich at Ivan's. I needed something the same, because I was scared. Betsy was pregnant. Martha was excited to be a grandma. But what would I be? Still a step-something-or-other or something real? I wanted Betsy to at least consider her options. She could go to trade school, earn a journeymen's license, do something besides clean houses.

But if the right accident happened to me, then maybe Betsy could quit next year. We could buy one of the subdivision houses, and she could stay at home, never have to bring the kid to work, where it would make paintbrushes and carpet scraps and bent nails into pretend families.

I tossed the rest of the sandwich and then dug around my truck bed until I found a tin of turpentine. I twisted off the lid, poured it down my arms, cupped it in my hands. My skin sizzled. The fumes burned my nose, and my stomach cartwheeled. I thought about what Hank had said about carpet glue, and I let the turpentine soak in until my skin blazed pink. I hopped back into my truck and drove to Doc Robby's without a seatbelt.

Doc Robby said he thought he'd fixed me up last time. I told him about the turpentine accident. He smiled and ushered me to the sink. We rinsed. So I told him my side hurt, maybe an exploding appendix. He said no, offered more Ameliorex. What about my lungs? Who knows what I'll cough up sucking so much paint. He said lungs were more resilient than most docs like to let on. They totally regenerate every seven years. But maybe—He said no.

Back at the subdivisions, I drove past one of the plumbers roughing copper in a trench. The trench walls started to cave in around him, and he winked at me, shrugged as the silt and clay enveloped his face. I kept on driving. The cream cheese and turkey roiled inside my belly. I punched my dash. Tomorrow he'd be able to walk through walls or spit copper pipe of perfect length. Things would be easier. I would just have the same miraculous regenerating lungs everyone else had.

The stonemasons careened across the sky and then gathered in a perfect V line. They were getting used to their wings. I sped to a cul-de-sac at the back of the sub, where the houses were finished and I could have some time alone to think among my white walls. But a truck was parked out front, and that meant there'd be handprints everywhere. Inside, I found Martha. From the entryway, I watched her over the half wall up the stairs. In one arm, she held a baby, and in the other, a spray bottle of blue cleaner. She squirted it at the window, and then the baby dabbed at it with its blanket. The baby left streaks.

"That baby's no good at cleaning windows," I said.

"He'll learn," Martha said. "This is his first one."

So he was a boy. A blank-slate baby boy. He could do any trade, master any tool. Maybe he'd paint with me. I'd be his mentor of all things white and wall. The thought helped me forget about Betsy, who'd forgone her options.

"Where's Betsy?" I stepped up one stair, closer to my wife and her grandchild.

"She left," Martha said. "Your shoes are filthy." The baby nodded his pink head.

I didn't have any paper booties, so I kicked off my shoes, lifted one up to investigate the bits of earth packed into the tread. They weren't that dirty.

"You know that ladders used to be the twelfth leading cause of injury in America?" Martha said.

"What changed?"

"Mostly extension ladders, though." She lifted the baby so he could reach the top of the window. He squeaked as if he was going to cry, scrunched up his face, but then found his smile.

"I mostly use stepladders." I peered inside my shoe for spots of blood, missing toes, anything.

Martha set the baby on the floor while she finished up. Her brown hair looked paler, and her few gray hairs blazed through the streakless window. The sun's stark shadows cast her worry lines deeper.

A stonemason flapped by and darkened the room.

Free from Martha's arms, the baby crawled for the stairs. It was a good thing I was at the bottom to catch him, and when I did, I'd let him hold my paintbrush. Before he had a chance to dive, a parade of trim-carpenter index fingers blocked the baby's path at the top of the stairs. They curled up and down, up and down, like a dance or some kind of warning. The baby raised one chubby pink hand and opened and closed it, opened and closed it.

I was never any good at reading body language. What I did know was those indexies weren't allowing my grandbaby to explore his world. If he wanted to go down the stairs, he had a damn right. He knew the risks: tumble and bump and crash. And he could clearly see me there waiting, no matter what decision he made, painter or plumber, electrician or roofer. If he fell and busted up, I'd take him somewhere better than Doc Robby.

The fingers curled faster. I wanted to jog up the steps and kick them all away. The baby swiped one up in his pink hand and jammed it into his mouth. All the other indexies inched away. The one in his mouth squirmed.

I opened up my arms for the baby to tumble into, but he just sucked that finger, gazing over my head at the flawless entryway wall I'd painted. It was perfectly untouched, as if no one had ever been there. That was me, my mark of nothing. I hoped the baby wouldn't choke.

ICE-CREAM DREAM

MANY ICE-CREAM TRUCKS TROLLED THE STREETS OF DEFIANCE, Ohio, but mine was the only modified 1986 Astro van painted beige with brown spots. My customers liked buying ice cream from a man popping his head out the side of a giraffe. They ran down the street, chasing my bumper, and I kept coasting at seven or eight miles an hour, my boot kissing the gas every now and then. A trail of kids lured more kids, who lured parents screaming for them to get out of the road. That mess made a crowd, and crowds meant business, and business meant I made rent and paid the electric bill and the gas bill and maybe even bought a new old movie from Lacy Stacy's Adult Boutique. But before I paid any of that, I'd drop fifty bucks into Roger and Frida's bank account. They came first, and they always will. Even if I never see them. Even though I can't pay child support, because their mother ran off with them when they were just learning to wobble on their stubby legs. A father doesn't stop loving his kids, no matter how long they don't know who the hell he is.

But as for all the boys not named Roger and all the girls not named Frida, they're all just little shits. Sometimes when I had five or six kids chasing the van, weaving in and out of my side-view mirror, I hovered my boot over the brake pedal. The pedal beckoned my foot, and I'd imagine hearing five or six kids pinging against the bumper. They'd get a big bite of steel. That would teach those little shits, who shoved sweaty crumples of money through the window, blocked the line while they jammed sweets down their throats, and then flicked their push-up sticks into my face. Some of them would take their Hippo-sicle and jet without paying. I wasn't fooled by a big smile missing two front teeth or mussed up golden locks or happy squints pocked with an adorable mess of freckles. There's no telling who's going to fuck you over.

My second week of ice-cream selling, I was driving down this real prime suburb just after dinner. Usually I'd have a dozen little shits chasing my bumper as I circled the cul-de-sacs, but all was silent. No kids playing on a single one of those sod lawns. Just me and the ice cream and my van tinkling "Flight of the Bumblebee." Every door was shut tight, every air conditioner humming away. Not an SUV creeping along the fresh blacktop. I was waiting for a goddamn tumbleweed to roll across the road.

Instead, in my side-view, a zebra-striped van appeared in the distance. I stuck my arm out the window, waved hello to my brother in arms, and he sped up, worn-out muffler roaring. The zebra van tinkled out "Camptown Races." Its tinny notes clashed with mine as it sucked up to my bumper. I pulled my arm back inside, kept driving, wondered if he needed to borrow some Sea Urchin Sammy Cream Pops. Just as I was counting inventory in my head, planning out a real nice gesture of sharing, another van appeared in my mirror, this one painted up like a dalmatian. It sped past the zebra van and sidled up next to me. It was tinkling some tune too, but at this point, I couldn't pick out one tune from another. It just sounded like a big pile of tinkles, like a swarm of fairies having an orgy. The dalmatian stayed tight on my side, and I waved again. I couldn't see inside the van, the side window tinted black as a missing tooth in a six-year-old's smile.

I sped up, tried to break away from these vans closing me in, mucking up my "Flight of the Bumblebee." The zebra behind accelerated right along with me, closer than ever, and the dalmatian to my side swerved into me until my rims ground the curb. I thought of Roger and Frida when they were toddlers. If their ball had skidded into the road, well, shit, there'd have been Roger and Frida pancakes. As much as I hated little shits, I couldn't live with their deaths caused by all us vans filling the street, flying through the suburbs at twenty-three miles per hour.

The subdivision exit appeared up ahead on my left, and soon I'd be on the main road and then the freeway and then back in my studio apartment watching *Selma Slams St. Louis* on my twenty-one-inch. I was ten yards away, when another van pulled out from behind a house, this one painted up like a cow and barreling straight at me.

They had me. Boxed me in and brought me to a stop. Next thing I knew, they'd yanked me out of my van and were kicking me in the head, pummeling me in the gut with ice-cream scoops. They worked quick and wore Jimmy Carter masks, so I couldn't get an ID on any of them. And I should've been figuring out how I'd survive this, but instead I wondered, just as the shortest Jimmy Carter ground his sneaker against my nose, where the hell they found Jimmy Carter masks. Nixon masks, sure. Reagan masks, no problem. But Jimmy C. didn't seem like a face that would demand a factory mold. I voted for him the day after Roger was born. We were busy with the new baby and scared as shit because we were just babies too, nineteen years old. But I made time to vote. Jimmy said he was going to make the country "competent and compassionate." A sweet baby like Roger needed competence and compassion. He deserved all of that. Frida came a year later, and two years after that, my ex stole them both away to Idaho. All the compassion in the world was sucked away, and I was left with a president who couldn't get a couple of his boys out of Iran. I was stuck working a shit job at the same go-nowhere freight yard where my father worked until he collapsed on a crate of duck-shaped pacifiers, dead instantly from a blood clot in his brain.

That scrawny Jimmy C. mask wearer gave me a final kick to the jaw. Of course the smallest guy would have to end things. It made me hope Roger had grown up to be a monstrous man who didn't need to prove shit, six and a half feet of confidence.

Those Jimmy Carters told me that I was entrepreneurializing on Scream-a-Dream Ice Cream turf, infringing copyrights with my unregistered animal van. They zip-tied my hands behind my back, jammed a map into my pocket. Then they tied me to a mailbox and pulled out knives. I'm not a man who's easily scared, but I'm also not an idiot who thinks he has a body made of steel and would talk shit to a glinting blade. I knew I could bleed, so I kept my mouth shut, watched silently when they slashed my tires and spray-painted STAY OFF SCREAM-A-DREAM TURF on the side of my van.

When they left, I tried to wriggle free, but I couldn't budge the ties, couldn't snap a tiny width of plastic. So I hung my head, leaned against the mailbox, resigned to stay there until some little shit found me and started pelting me with stones. I didn't have to wait. The mailbox snapped under my weight. It wasn't my muscle or my ingenuity that freed me, but all those pounds I'd put on since I stopped working the freight yards.

I called a tow. I got home. Didn't need no damn emergency room, just a microwave salisbury steak and a movie. Before I watched, I double-checked the back of the *Selma Slams St. Louis* box for the date. I didn't watch anything that came out after 1995. Frida turned eighteen in 1997, and I added two years, just to be safe. Every father prays his daughter doesn't get into that kind of acting, but I wasn't around to raise her right. There's just no telling. Selma donned her heels and G-string in 1985. She made me feel safe, banging dozens of men in a time before Frida would have grown to learn the incompetence and cruelty of this world.

I scrubbed blood out of my shirt while Selma moaned. I'd taken worse beatings. Before a tiny curdle of blood killed my dad, he spent years thrashing me with the rubber insoles of his work boots. I don't know why he used the insoles. All that matters is he was a cruel asshole, slapping the foot stink of an eight-hour all over my face.

I spread the map those Scream-a-Dream bastards gave me across my kitchen counter. Every halfway decent suburb in town was highlighted in blood-red ink—Scream-a-Dream turf. They left me freeways and industrial districts and dirt roads on the county line. I took the giraffe van out on the road the next day, thinking about all the places I couldn't go. A free man in an unfree country, an anchor the size of Toledo tied to my bumper. How was I ever going to make enough money to give Roger and Frida the life they deserved? When I drove to one of my designated work zones, the freight yards over by the Maumee River, I considered spinning the wheel, aiming my van at the bridge guardrails, and barreling through. At least Roger and Frida would collect the life insurance policy. And then they'd know my name, know their real daddy. Only, I didn't know their names. The ex could've remarried. Any name could've landed in their laps. Any faceless man could be the one they called Daddy.

I didn't drive the giraffe over the bridge. The Maumee smelled like shit, and that's no way to drown, lungs filled with brown water all foamed up by melting ice cream. I drove past the subdivisions where I couldn't go, my tinkler silent. I listened out the window for the sounds of my competition but heard nothing, and what a damn shame that I couldn't work the routes they weren't even using. I was about to say fuck it and drive into a no-no zone called Emerald Pines, when I spotted a subdivision with no name out front.

The blacktop was fresh, smooth and black. Not a house in sight. After a quarter mile of gnarled brush lining the curbs, they finally appeared. But not the clean vinyl-and-brick facades of the usual subdivision houses. The birth of new construction was an ugly sight. These houses wore siding like scabs, speckling the nakedness of plastic house wrap. Deeper into the subdivision, I watched two-by-four skeletons cast their stringy shadows onto the parched dirt. Or no skeletons at all, only holes in the ground where houses might grow. No families here, no little shits—no place a Scream-a-Dream van would ever stalk. Instead of painted-up tinkling vans, plain white ones littered the curbs, ladders strapped to their roofs. Or half-ton pickup trucks, their beds spilling scaffolding and sheets of drywall and copper wires and brass pipes. And all around me, grizzled men stared, aimed their unshaven chins at my van, gripped their shovels and nail guns tighter.

Now, if I were a Scream-a-Dream sucker, I would've whipped my van into a U-turn and zipped out of there, dragging my zebra tail between my rear axle. But this challenge of entrepreneurship made my heart race, my teeth itch, fingers tap-tapping the steering wheel. No little shits as far as the eye could see, but there was potential here. I flicked on "Flight of the Bumblebee" and slowed the van to a creep. The men who hadn't looked before did so now, craning their necks from ladders, hammers halted in midswing. I kept my eyes straight ahead, focused on the work of keeping my foot just barely pressed against the gas, tried to forget about my van that could've hauled lumber but was painted like a giraffe, tried to forget about my flabby biceps, my soft hands. But I'd put in my time at the freight yards, lifting crates until my arms burned.

I heard a yelp, and when I looked into my side-view, I saw one of the workers following me. He wore a baby-blue polo shirt a size too small so that the bare bottom of his belly wiggled brightly as he jogged behind me. His tool belt jangled with the rattle of nails and hammers. I fought the urge to press the brake. One frenzied customer could easily turn into two, two into four, four into a snaking tail of hot and hungry men dying for my ice cream.

But no one else picked up after the fat man in the polo. The road ended in a cul-de-sac, and I parked. The man jogged up to the side window where I kept the menu. He planted both hands on the van, gasping and studying.

I slid out of my seat, withheld opening the side window as long as I could. A customer waiting to order was the start to a crowd of followers. I opened my coolers, took a quick stock of my Quintuple-Berry Pops, pulled a roll of small bills from my pocket, and then, finally, slowly slid the window open.

"Christ on a stick, you nearly killed me." His chest heaved. He licked his lips. "I'm going to need an IV of Fudge-O-Saurus Bars stat."

I spread ten bars across the counter and smiled.

"How fat do you think I am, asshole?" he said. "They'll saw off my left foot if I eat all of those."

I moved to pull them away, and he grabbed my wrist, said, "Shit. I have some hungry boys back at the house. I guess I can put them to use."

He gave me a fifty, told me to keep the change, and the profits there were ten bucks in the kids' account and half an *Annie Poke-Me* video.

After the fat man left, I was alone again. I needed to get rid of my stock soon, or it would start to get freezer burn, and then I'd have to eat the loss. Except I couldn't eat the loss literally. I'm lactose intolerant, ever since I was a kid. When my daddy used to take me to get ice cream after laying into me with his boot insoles, it just meant more punishment. Knots in my belly, welts on my back, a night spent curled over the toilet crying, and that would just get the old man all fired up with the insoles again for my being an ungrateful little shit.

The tinkler ran through a half-dozen more rounds of its tune before I heard a knock at the window. Two men stood outside, picking flakes of drywall mud off their shirts. They asked me if I had any water, and I didn't, but I told them how refreshing a Weasel Pop could be. They shelled out a couple bucks, and then one of them said, "Now, if you had water in there, you could make a killing."

The other one, whose baseball cap barely fit over a mess of curly brown hair, said, "Or if you had a shitter we could use, guys around here would pay for that. You get a little tired of shitting in buckets."

I didn't have the heart to try to sell them more ice cream after hearing that, especially with my own lactose-intolerant stomach twitching just feet away from freezers full of torture. But they got me thinking. If life hands you lemons, you don't have to make lemonade. You sell those lemons for better product. Or you carve those lemons into bowls made of rind or into little lemon hats for dogs, or you pelt the giver of lemons with his own lemons until he relents and gives you oranges. Life is full of lemon givers, and a smart man takes his fate and makes more than just complacent lemonade. Those tradesmen, for example, had pockets full of cash yet no water to drink, no proper pot to piss in. But they had plenty of buckets, and they made that work. They had new sinks and copper pipes to install but no water. Now they had me, who could provide life's simple necessities.

Before I went home that night, I stocked up the van. That man with that mess of curls stuck in my head at the store, haunting me through the aisles, tugging at my pant legs, saying, *I want this. I need that.* And when I showed up the next day, I had ice-cold water and beer and sandwiches and cigarettes and, sorry, though, no solution for the bucket issue. What I did have was barber scissors, and for twenty bucks, they could eat a sandwich, drink a beer, and get their hair cut. I remember working the freight yards; by the time you clocked out, all the barbers were closed. Curly's paychecks probably went straight to the bartender, because no one else was open.

Within a few weeks, I was banking more than I'd ever made hawking ice cream to little shits. Roger and Frida's bank account swelled up, and I had a queue of classic videos from Lacy Stacy's stacked on my VCR.

And the workers, my boys, I was so proud of them. Through the weeks of my visits, those holes in the ground bloomed. Those boys took the materials stacked in their truck beds and built full-fledged homes, easy as Lincoln Logs. They couldn't have done it so fast without me there to hydrate and feed them, to take care of their every need. They loved me for what I provided them, and I loved them for loving me. We were happy.

One day, a few weeks in, I was trimming Julius's brown curls, him straddling a sawhorse, me smiling over top of his lush, sawdust-filled locks. It was lunchtime, so a dozen of the other young men lounged around the van, sipping beers, licking Freedom Cones, gnawing my homemade egg-salad sandwiches. In the distance, I heard a familiar tinkling. The long-healed bruises on my skull pulsed anew. I tried to hide it from my boys, but my grinding teeth betrayed me, flashed my anxiety like an insole welt to the forehead. They huddled around me, offered sips from their beers. Julius tipped his head back, stared me right in the eyes, and once he got a look at whatever showed on my face, he reached back and patted my arm, nodded.

The zebra van rolled into view, slowed near the finished houses. Finished but not sold, not yet full of little shits. This was still a place for young workingmen. My customers. The boys mingling around me crossed their arms, snarled their lips at the van. All except Wilson, the one who'd chased me the first day, the biggest man on-site. I couldn't blame him for the hunger he bore deep in his endless gut. He sprinted after that zebra van, yelled, "I scream for ice cream, boys!" And the boys around me shook their heads, said, "Fuck him, Mr. Denning. That stupid fat ass can't find his own dick, let alone a sense of loyalty."

And I said, "I don't mind, fellas." Because I knew he was young. They were grown men but still boys in so many ways, still guided by flitting wants. The long term was eons away.

The zebra van slowed, parked, and Wilson ran up to the side. He spread his thick fingers across the window, peered inside, rapped on the glass. And I thought that was fine, just fine. A man can't hold on to his customers any more than he can hold on to anything he loves in this world. If you love something, let it go, and all that.

The zebra stripes started to quaver, bounced slightly up and down. I wondered if maybe the van was rumbling on a bad engine. The stripes bounced more, and then the tires facing me left the ground for the briefest of seconds. Wilson wasn't waiting for ice cream; he was pushing the van, rocking it back and forth. Three more boys from Wilson's framing crew sprinted toward the van, hammers waving above their heads. They pounded against the zebra stripes, the ring of steel on aluminum drowning out the tinkle of "Camptown Races." Soon, more boys ran toward the truck. The ones who'd stayed by me, who'd crossed their arms and rebuked Wilson, now smiled like children, sprinted toward the van, until it was swarmed by men, swinging their tools, rocking the van with their grime-smeared arms, work boots dug in to the hot blacktop.

I thought I heard a squeal and like to imagine that was my competition inside shrieking in fear. The van stuttered forward, pushed out of the mob of my boys and out of my subdivision.

Julius leaned back on the sawhorse, pointed at the van. "We only need one ice-cream man."

The men chased the van as far as they could, until it rolled out of sight and the air grew silent. The back of Julius's head faced me, so he didn't see the tears I held back. I think he knew how I felt, though, when he said, "A little more off the top, old man."

But nothing lasts forever. The SALE PENDING signs popped up, and the trucks and white vans drove onward. They didn't tell me where they were going next, just nodded their trimmed heads and shoved off. Maybe they thought I knew where they were going. Maybe they figured the world was full of men like me who could take care of them. Providers are just supposed to be there. I tried not to resent them, tried to understand that's just how it goes.

One crew remained, though. The painting-touch-up crew was always the last to leave. They had a final day of work left and two haircutting appointments with me. I was sure one of them would invite me to the next site, tell me how much my van meant to them, beg me to follow them forever. I hopped into the giraffe van, the morning sun gleaming up those glorious last strands of fraying hope. I smiled and turned the key, thinking about Roger and Frida and how they could be as close as a plane ticket, when I got smacked in the temple.

I came to in the back of my van, arms tied behind my back, three Jimmy Carter masks staring at me. A fourth Carter sat in the driver's seat. It was one thing to knock me around but quite another to drive another man's giraffe. So I kicked the closest Carter in the groin and tried to scramble to my feet. They shoved me back on my ass, and the Carter I kicked laid into my back with the ice-cream scoop.

Once he tuckered out, I said, "All right, boys, what could possibly be the problem now? I'm off your turf. I did everything you asked, much as it hurt my pride."

"We're claiming new turf," the biggest one said. "We claim all suburbs. There's no more need for your freezer-burned products."

That got the heat burning into my face. I'd never sold a bite of freezer-burned ice cream to any customer and never would. But I fought back the anger riling inside me.

"No business there but workingmen. They hardly buy enough ice cream for me to pay insurance on my van."

"Been selling more than that." The Carter I'd kicked picked up my barber shears, snipped twice at the air. "And I don't remember us giving you permission to sell products outside the ice-cream family."

Those air snips didn't intimidate me. I gave up asking for permission a long time ago, after my daddy died in a box of pacifiers and after I quit living in his work boots, clocking in and out of the freight yards. I rushed the Carters, slammed headfirst into that bastard snipping my barber shears. We fell to the floor, me on top, him screaming like a little shit who'd just dropped his Super Dipper Cone. I didn't see what all the screaming was about. I've become a husky man, but short, not the kind of frame that could carry scream-inducing weight. A young fellow should be able to take a blow and wear a bruise like a man. My daddy taught me that lesson my whole life.

I rolled free of the screaming Carter and waited for the others to pound on me again. But they stood there, toothy Carter smiles gawking down at us. And the one just kept on whining. The orange handles of my scissors jutted from his gut, made him look like one of those toys you wind up.

The Carters hovering over us wheezed through their breathing holes. Their eyes flitted behind molds of shiny rubber. Finally, one of them nodded and then whispered into the driver's ear. The van slowed. I stared at the stabbed Carter writhing on my van's floor, a trickle of blood streaming toward the freezer. I only looked up once I heard the door slide open. The Carters jumped out, tucked and rolled as if they evacuated moving vans every day. The front door popped open, and out went the driver. They all jumped ship, left their little friend to bleed out in my truck.

The van crept along unmanned. Just as I scrambled to the front seat, the van smacked into a telephone pole. I sat behind the wheel, staring at the pole, waiting for it to snap and crash down on top of us. The van had stalled out, and I listened to the cooling engine. Tick-tick-tick. The pole didn't budge. So I had to decide what to do next. And sometimes the world is like that. Sometimes it's not as easy as getting smashed by a telephone pole.

That bleeding bastard in the back hollered worse. He'd rolled over onto the shears and switched from shrieking to sniffling, moaning for his momma between sucking snot through his mask's breathing holes. Why doesn't anyone ever call for their daddy when getting stabbed with barber shears?

I started up the van. The hospital was only a few miles away. I could drop him off and still make my appointment with the painting crew, if I hurried. The telephone pole had cracked the windshield; two streaking lines shaped into a Y, two skinny arms reaching out from a center. The tinkler wouldn't shut off, kept bleating the same first dozen notes of "Flight of the Bumblebee" over and over again. Each time it restarted, which was every two seconds, the bleeding Carter in the back howled.

I couldn't just drop moaning, bleeding Carter at the front door of the emergency room. My busted-up giraffe kept spewing an insane flurry of incomprehensible notes. Not much of a getaway vehicle. So I pulled up to the back of the hospital, slid open the door, and rolled Carter's slumped body to the strip of grass between road and parking lot.

Just as his body tumbled out, he got some fight back in him, said, "Fuck you, old man."

I laughed, standing over him, me safe in my giraffe and him bleeding out in the grass. Just goes to show that the man who seeks his manifest destiny beats the man who stumbles along as a follower, wearing a mask, cowering in the crowd. You see where it got him. Whereas, I was free to continue on, making a difference for my working boys and supporting my babies, who were no longer babies. No longer babies but full-grown people who probably called some insurance salesman named Bob, Dad.

I drove onward to my appointment with the painting boys, toward—I don't know. Freedom, money, the American dream. A giraffe and a broken song and a van full of ice cream. Carter had called me "old man." If I was old, how old was he? Where did he come from? Anyone could hide behind that mask. And maybe a kid with spunk like his would've left Bob the insurance salesman's home and struck out on his own. Maybe he'd hit the open road, seeking to feel the hot blood of freedom pumping through his rebellious veins, that blood now dripping through blades of hospital sod.

I turned back toward the hospital, left the painting boys wearing their hair long. They'd keep building houses, keep moving, find their own needs. When I got back to the parking lot, no one had found Carter yet. It was me or nobody. I parked, left the engine running, stepped toward the crumpled body in the grass. He was still moaning but quieter now, a guttural lullaby. He didn't swear at me when my body cast a shadow over him. I knelt, slid my arm under his neck. He was all Carter from the neck up, but through the rubber eyeholes, brown—like millions of others' eyes but like mine, too. I slipped my fingers under Carter's chin, felt the tight skin of a young man underneath. The sandpaper of two days of stubble, a man who didn't care about being clean shaven, about strangling himself with a tie in a cubicle. I pulled back the rubber mask to his lips and then stopped. I would see this man's face soon, after I took him inside, paid his hospital bill with Roger and Frida's savings account. And then I'd know. This young man could sit in the passenger seat, learn the true meaning of freedom, see a man run his own business. He could follow my path to freedom, a path that didn't need a past, only a will to drive down any new road, still soft with fresh blacktop, the tires sticking at first but then pulling free.

WE RIDE BACK

OUR VAN SWERVES THE SUBDIVISION CURVES, IN AND OUT OF cul-de-sacs. The moon blares, white and shiny as our van. We are invisible in this gleaming box. We look like workers. Workers look like us. We can sneak in and steal all we deserve.

The back has no seats. Ribs and Lizzy bounce and bobble across the cold metal floor. Ribs stands, braces, pressing his palms against the walls. His long arms stretched, he looks like a skeleton Jesus, thin layer of skin and T-shirt over those jutting ribs. So many damn ribs. Lizzy's balled in the back corner. Trying to stay so small she can't fall.

Cal aims us square at a mailbox but pulls left just in time. Tires squeal. Van lurches. Ribs and Lizzy thud against the right wall. Cal can't keep his big horse teeth in his mouth, laughing it up while we risk blowing cover. What the hell's the point of finding a white van as invisible as a workingman's van, then? Why the hell go begging Lizzy's ex-stepdad to ask his new brother-in-law, Stew, to borrow one off his used-as-shit bad-loan lot? And Lizzy had to act all cute, leaning over his desk and flashing down her low-cut shirt and talking baby voice. That used to be her dad in a way, and that's something just not right. But a stepdad ain't a dad-dad—our stepkids never let us forget that.

We slap Cal's head for wasting Lizzy's cleavage. Time to drive straight and be hidden and aim for the houses in the back that are getting built. Ones where no people live. No families yet.

Not like that one with the light glaring upstairs and a shadow of a kid staring through lacy curtains. That kid looks like he's looking at us. We don't want that. We want scabbed siding, gravel lawns, garage doors like gaping black mouths. Houses where people work instead of live. Houses like where we used to work before they stopped making families to make houses to make work.

Cal parks the van. We tumble out. Ribs hurls. Lizzy laughs. Cal pisses in the moonlight. We scope out this back cul-de-sac. Four half-finished houses. We each pick one and split.

In the dark, alone, wearing all black, we wait for our eyes to adjust. Our bodies feel like nothing. Lighter than Ribs's rail-thin frame. We cough or clear our throats or giggle or tap our teeth just to be sure we haven't turned shadow. We rub our thighs, pinch our necks. When we're certain we're here, no fooling, we hunt.

We hunt closets. We hunt basements. We hunt cabinets and garages and behind the furnace. We hunt alone, but there's Lizzy's flashlight sparking up the basement window next door, or maybe that's Cal's house. Neighbors of the absent. Not so much alone as apart. Not so much apart as departmentalized, delegated, defined by what we don't do anymore, defined by what we find. And we find lots.

We hug armloads of hand tools, shiny and Stanley. Ribs drags a compressor heavy enough to rip his sparrow bones. Cal says he's got the motherfucking mother lode back in his master bedroom walk-in. Lizzy says screw that. She found a score under the drops in her garage. This sub has never been hit, we realize. This sub is full of trust. Workers who never had to rebuy their tools from the pawnshop. Workers who never hit famine, only feast.

Tile saw, table saw, miter saw, nailers, and two hundred squares of oak tongue and groove from Lizzy. Three cordless radios and a Honda generator from Cal. Ribs thinks he doesn't have nothing worth taking. Ribs says his stuff is too dirty and beat-up, but we know better. Ribs found himself a painters' stash: Graco gas-powered sprayer, HVLP with two guns, buckets of brushes, enough extensions poles and ladders to extend across the sub. All of it paint speckled to hell. But Lizzy isn't afraid of dirty. She spent three years painting for her stepdad's best friend, Big Dave. But she got tired of him snapping her bra and peeking up her shirt when she was way up the ladder. So one day, she kicked out his ladder legs.

We pack up the van as fast as we can, because Cal is getting twitchy. He keeps scratching his neck, grinding his teeth, saying how he sure as shit won't get popped on parole. We let him worry. Worry makes him fast, even though he loads like an angry-drunk garbageman. Crash goes a nailer. Fuck you, claw hammer. What are you looking at, Sawzall? We want to hush him, but we don't. We know about his four hungry babies at home. About his twenty years swinging hammer and then fired and nothing. No 401(k)s for us. No pension. Not a damn thing on paper. So, yeah, fuck those bosses and these bosses and everyone who can afford these tools.

The van fills too fast, and we'll have to ditch the oak tongue and groove. Cal heaves a last bucket of hand tools into the van, lets whatever can fit crash in the nooks, and the rest clinks to the concrete. Down the street, five houses blaze up. Families waking. Families getting wise, knowing no workers work this late. Cal slams the back doors, and when they don't shut, he rams with his shoulder. He slides into the driver's side door, hollers, Hurry the fuck up.

Just one seat left on the passenger side. Even the space between the front bucket seats is crammed with drill cases. A good haul. Too good. No room for us. Not all of us gonna ride tonight, Cal says. Sorry, Ribs, Cal decides. I mean, just tough luck for now is all, Cal hums. Cal's logic: Ribs can risk. Ribs has no priors, and he can walk, and we'll pay him when we meet up again, in Lizzy's parking lot. Right? Cal says. I mean, right?

Ribs balls his fists, eyes wide, whites glowing in the moon. Sirens in the distance. Maybe those sirens sing for us, maybe not.

True, Ribs has no priors. But Ribs is so skinny. Ribs is gypsum dust blowing away in the breeze. Ribs is a baby, not even twenty, and so full of poke marks and purple blotches. Too much.

Lizzy climbs in. Her van. Her spot guaranteed. Cal is revving the engine, pointing. Right? he repeats. Right? Just one spot left. I push Ribs inside, close the door. They skid off, and I hightail it through the yard. I've got priors. I've screwed up many times. But I don't shoot up. I don't have any habit anymore but a ten-year-old named Lucinda. I don't have a job, but I run every day, three miles, five miles. Sometimes I just run and run around my block until my legs melt. It feels like work, something like what I used to do. And now all that running means something. I sprint into the next yard, weave saplings, hurdle bushes, hop fences. Lights flick on, but I disappear just as fast. Into another yard and another, chasing darkness.

Those sirens are for me for sure now. Coming and coming. I'm so close, nearing the edge of the houses, the road ahead. I roll into a ditch, duck, wait while the sirens pour into the sub. Ribs and Lizzy and Cal are long gone. And no one will find me. Because I left the work of stealing work. I'm here, crouched, hiding, spying my way out. Above me, that still-lighted window watches. That shadow kid gazes out of lace curtains, peeking out of his warm room and trying to imagine a world outside. And I hope that kid takes forever to figure out that what's outside is empty, is invisible in the night, is me.

THE SHEPHERD'S WORK

WHEN REN TOLD MAGGIE HE'D TRIPLE MORTGAGED THEIR hovel to buy twenty acres of bluestem grass for his fourteen sheep, she hacked off her curly blonde ponytail and threw it in his porridge. "Might as well take this, too," she said. He should've started by telling her how his life had changed, how he'd become a better businessman, hence a better all-around man, hence a better potential father, and all for the price of admission to the weekend shepherding seminar, Baba in the Black. The host, Tommy Two Bags of Wool, had swooped his purple robe like a magician upon entering the stage. He'd told the audience, "It's not just your sheep that are your sheep—though your sheep are your primary sheep. You must dream big, guide the arms of your loved ones—who are your secondary, metaphorical sheep—into the extra-large sweater sleeves of a better, woollier future."

Maggie turned her face to the front door, and Ren plucked her ponytail from his breakfast and sucked the strands clean. He snuck her hair into the robe pocket nearest his heart. Her newly bobbed hair quivered as she pulled her oversweater over her undersweater and then disappeared out the door. He liked Maggie's hair short. It reminded him of the second week after shearing season, when

89

they had coin to spend and budding curls replaced naked, scabbed sheep flesh. But the extra coin always ran out quickly.

Ren had staked his land, his right to a better, woollier future. It wasn't just for him but for Maggie, for the family they'd been trying to make for years. Ren would fill their pockets with coin and make them rich and happy, and Maggie's belly would balloon. Their perfect future sprang easy as dandelions from his newer, better grass.

Ren grabbed his staff and headed to the sheep pen and led his fourteen sheep the three miles to his new rolling hills of green. Green like Maggie's eyes, which shimmered most in the electricity of twilight, as on the days when he used to return from shepherding and she'd be waiting, her naked thighs leaning against the glowing threshold of their home. Her thighs never awaited him now that she part-timed at her brother's flute shop. That could change soon.

The new field dipped into a basin guarded by gray slate walls that blocked the western wind. A stream trickled from the east, and it sounded like diamonds tinkling into a woolen sack. Ren guessed that's what it sounded like. He'd never actually heard diamonds tinkling, nor had he seen a diamond. He had seen sheep molars. And now he listened to them grinding, grass turning to mush, sliding down throats. The song of profit. The whisper of coat growth only a fifth-generation shepherd could decipher.

Shepherding was in his blood. Thanks, Papa Ander. Thanks, Grandpa Nork. Their inept philosophy of sitting and twiddling thumbs and waiting for the flock to flourish to that impossible goal of twenty sheep had led to this moment of perfect evolution, this moment when Ren would realize their failed dreams. Now that he had the land, the lambs would come. Winona, his head ewe, chewed steadily.

Ren plopped onto a boulder, took a deep breath of his sweet new future, and thought about Maggie. Soon she'd be rolling naked through seas of fresh wool. Her fingers would be smooth again, freed from the calluses of flute carving, and she'd run them over his chin, down his sternum, past his waist, curl his red pubic hair.

Ren pulled the side of his robe over his erection. But he was alone in the vast basin. He threw back his robe and allowed his erection to jettison upward, the same direction his business would grow.

Ren gazed over his basin, imagined wobbling newborn lambs, could almost hear the tinny jingle of their bells. The jingle grew into a clanging. The lambs stumbled out of his dream. Over the crags of the basin, a man waved a stubby sword. He wore a rusty breastplate, chain mail gauntlets, was barefooted and mud smeared. Their eyes met, and the shoddy soldier sprinted toward him. Ren reclosed his robe.

"Did I miss it?" the soldier asked. Ren studied the man's mud-kissed chubby cheeks, dopey eyes, blond fuzz over his lip. He was nothing but a child of a man. "Am I late for battle? Fighting for the honor of Finneus the Third's land, slayer of giant salamanders."

"I think you've lost your way, son," Ren said.

"Thank the fifteen and a half gods above, then. I'm on time. Fuck's sake, I'd say I'm early." He sheathed his sword.

"This is grazing land." Ren leaned sagely against his staff. "There's no battle to worry about. You can run along."

"Nope." The soldier pushed his fists into his back and swung his hips, stretching. "This has always been the place."

More clanging rang from the basin lip. Another man emerged, waving a halberd.

"Time for me to die a glorious death, pops." The young soldier rushed toward the other man. Their weapons crashed just past Ren's sheep Franklin. Franklin bleated at the men, trotted back and forth. Ren rushed toward the squabble but stopped when an arrow hissed into the earth in front of his sandals. Along the basin lip, a dozen archers drew their bows, let arrows sail. There were only two men with Ren in the basin. Wasted feathers and flint and wood. Tommy Two Bags of Wool would have had a good laugh at their foolish budgeting of resources.

More breastplates and muddy faces and swords and maces crested the lip. They shouted as they loped down the hills, hurdling Ren's sheep. The sheep stared with slack jaws, black lips curled and raised from the grass. They couldn't concentrate, thus couldn't eat, thus wouldn't reach lamb-conceiving romance.

Arrows split the earth around Ren. His sheep remained frozen, watching the men, transfixed, orange eyes glazed. He prodded Whitey's yellowed rear, jabbed his staff between Franklin's eyes. Nothing. Ren's stomach twisted. The breeze blew cold beneath his frock.

His fingers twitched around his staff. He thought about the clowder of flame-red bobcats that had eaten two of his ewes three years ago. He remembered the drop in his groin when he'd stumbled on to the ewe carcasses, bellies torn open and emptied. Maggie had wanted him to quit. But Ren fought back. The next time the clowder lurked into his herd, he'd pounced in front of them. He became huge and loud, a big show of screaming and flailing, a bigger show than even Tommy Two Bags could perform. The bobcats ran away as easy as that, at the mere show of danger.

He channeled that bobcat battle now. He screamed and growled, spit frothing over his lips. He twirled the staff over his head, swung blindly at the wind. His throat burned, and his ears buzzed. He charged at the man-boy soldier, who lay on the ground, bracing his sword against halberd strikes from a larger warrior. The man-boy winced toward Ren, eyebrows raised, a slice in his cheek leaking a trickle of red. The man-boy looked tired, older, transformed into an ancient visage of scowling fear.

A sliver of pity wormed into Ren's chest. He latched his crook around the halberd and yanked it to the grass. The larger warrior ran away. The archers screeched like a murder of magpies and disappeared over the hill. Ren's land became all green again except for a few glints of blade and arrowhead. The shoddy man-boy raised himself onto his elbows and curled his lips into a yellow-toothed smile.

"Hell if you ain't the savior of the giant salamander–slayer clan, mister." The man-boy reached his bloody palm toward Ren. "My ancestor's would bless you, if they weren't all dead and rotted."

Ren offered the man-boy his crook and pulled him to his feet. "I don't need your blessings."

"My children's runts will sing your praise."

"And I don't need any songs. Just peace and quiet for my sheep so they can make lambs."

"That how it's done? Just leave 'em alone? The wenches in town would be pleased as shit to hear that." The man-boy laughed, clapped Ren's shoulder. "Whatever you want, friend. You're a piece of my freaking heart now. All will know who won back the land of my father's father, slayer of Mighty Francis the Stump Plucker."

"This isn't your father's land. I bought it."

"Sure, Shepherd. We've won. You can graze here until the cows come home."

"Sheep."

"Sheep or cows or anteaters. Whatever you want, brother." The man-boy pounded his chest and then slapped Ren's. The man-boy departed toward the basin lip. At the slate crest, he hollered, "See you tomorrow."

Before Ren could protest, the man-boy soldier was gone. He tried not to think about what tomorrow could mean while he wandered through the field, plucking arrow shafts. Across the basin, he noticed Franklin's head dipped to the ground, still eating, and Ren was glad. At least one sheep would grow strong, would father fine lambs. When he neared, he saw that Franklin was licking a puddle of blood, his muzzle streaked pink, pink darkening to brown. He imagined lambs covered in tainted brown wool, stupid and dirty and worthless.

For just one moment, he allowed himself to miss his old half-acre plot, the sprouts of crab grass and pocks of dandelions. Maggie used to bring him lunch there. Her hair long and full of tangles from sleep, she'd recline in his lap, and he'd work a brush through her hair. They'd watch the sheep forage, and it was good. But that wasn't production.

Maggie needed to know that her brother wasn't the only success. Ren couldn't just sit around combing hair, waiting for wool to grow. He fingered Maggie's hacked-off ponytail coiled at the bottom of his pocket. It would sustain him until things took off and she could quit the flute business and join him on the new land with his giant herd. One day in the future, he'd gift this chopped lock back to her, and she'd laugh and her face would redden. He'd tell her about these men playing war, and she'd laugh at that too, one day.

Darkness settled as Ren led his sheep two miles out of their way, to Tommy Two Bags of Wool's cave. Why build an office, Tommy always said, when God leases caves? Caves saved on overhead. Ren pushed aside the vines covering the cave mouth, cleared his throat, said, "You open, Tommy?"

"A real business never closes. Sleep is for the unemployed, the retired, and the dead." Tommy sprang from the darkness. "What can I do for my favorite shepherd?"

Tommy neared Ren as he spoke, almost touching his chin to Ren's chest. Ren smelled fish and rhubarb on his breath, could see a pus-filled growth on his tongue when he licked at his red mustache. At the conference, he'd looked majestic under the lights of the stage from ten rows away.

"You sold me some bunk acres. There're a bunch of idiots fighting there."

"You're imagining things." Tommy's eyes glared wetly in the moonlight. "You just need to change your visualization techniques. Daily success-envisionment meditation with my eight-part series of motivational tapes will change those fears into fantastic."

"My eyes aren't the problem."

"Ah, yes, it's the classic overworked-shepherd syndrome. You should try my patent-pending Calmative Cave Mushroom Caps. Relax you into oblivion. But they'll keep you sharp, too." The lesion on Tommy's tongue flickered as he spoke. "Bottom-dollar deal."

"I don't need mushrooms." Ren withdrew the arrow shaft he'd brought and lifted it to Tommy's face. "I'm not imagining anything."

Tommy snatched the arrow, pressed it to his nose, slid his tongue down the shaft. Then he chucked it over his shoulder, into the black cave.

"I appreciate you forwarding this concern to my attention." Tommy gripped Ren's shoulders. "You need to look at those salamander boys as an obstacle to overcome, an opportunity to improve your strategy. They are a gift." Tommy released Ren's shoulder. He pulled at his mustache. "But if it's too much for you to handle, I can refund you two-thirds."

"Why not all thirds?"

"The price of doing business," Tommy said. "Or I could sell you some different acres for a few hundred extra. These ones are perfect and obstacle-opportunity free."

Maggie's brother could loan Ren the money, would insist on no interest and that would be so much worse. Maggie and Flann would laugh about listening to wool grow, while they sweated out five thousand more flute shafts, while they took lunch break and played with Flann's three boys and two girls, and before break was over, Flann's wife would pop out another son.

"I'm not buying more land. I just need a safe, quiet place so my herd can make lambs."

Tommy snickered. "You should consider taking my lambing class, Mary Had a Little Lamb and so Can You."

Ren reached into his pocket and twisted Maggie's hair tightly around his thumb. Tommy smirked at him and then disappeared into his cave's darkness. He rattled in the gulf of shadows and finally emerged holding out his palm. "Tell you what. A quick and easy fix. This will solve all your problems."

Ren looked down and, to his horror, saw a flute. But this one was different than the ones Flann and Maggie made. Its metal shaft glinted in the moonlight. This was a flute Flann would have no idea how to craft. Ren loosened the noose of Maggie's hair around his thumb.

"Next time you run into trouble, just give this sucker a blow, and poof, your worries will be eradicated. All for a low-low investment."

"What's the price?"

"Low-low *investment*, my wise friend. Not a single coin, but a barter." Tommy's tongue flicked fast, seemed to brighten his face, so that Ren could see his sharp cheekbones, the wisdom lines in his forehead. "All I require is just one sheep."

Ren needed another investment, and he could spare Franklin, surely, who was full of soldier blood and stupidity. So he made the exchange. Ren crooked the sheep and led him into Tommy's cave. Tommy slipped the shiny flute into Ren's pocket. When he withdrew his hand, Tommy was holding Maggie's hair.

"Oh, this is a fine coat from a rare sheep." Tommy smiled, rubbed the hair against his cheek. "Let's toss this into the exchange."

Ren yanked the hair from Tommy and stowed it back in his pocket. He clutched her hair in a fist as he departed. Now he had Maggie, his new land, and the flute that would fix everything else.

Maggie was sleeping by the time Ren found his way to their bed. One of her hands lay splayed next to the uneven chunks of hair on the back of her head. Red slices and brown scabs flecked her fingers, casualties of flute work. He pulled Maggie's hair from his pocket and swept the curls over the wounds, because the right hair cured all that ailed. He believed that as hard as he'd ever believed anything.

She snorted in her sleep, and her hand disappeared beneath the wool blankets. Blankets made of his sheep. He pinched a loose thread hanging from the hem, imagined Winona's haunches. Soon, once he had peace on his new land, he would have dozens of Winona's daughters, all with fine wool, and he'd save all the softest hair to make blankets just for Maggie. So many blankets she'd never know cold again. Only warmth. A womb of wool. So many blankets. But then she'd never need his body heat, unlike the winters they'd spent when all they had was the one threadbare quilt. Back then they would drag that quilt to the stove, pull it tight around their toes, their legs twined, arms quivering until their shared body heat meshed and the shivering stopped and then they made love, softly at first, slow hip thrusts so as not to break from the blanket. And then Maggie would become daring, roll on top of him, yank off her sweater, and escape from the quilt, her bare breasts glowing in the frigid moonlight.

Cold became another kind of touch then. Sweat stilled over goosebumps. Movement of hips and arms and bodies pressed, until heat wasn't a thing to be kept in a blanket or locked in the stove but a burning between their waists that could fill a cold and empty house.

But their heat never filled anything. Her belly never grew. And now they each had separate thick woolen blankets.

Soon, soon, they would have more wool and more money, and that would bring Maggie back inside his blanket. He'd pay off the mortgages and build a second-story add-on to their hovel. She'd be comfortable and safe, and they would make love with precision and purpose. That would work. That would have to work.

Maggie's tired arms and scraped hands stretched across the mattress. Ren would need to push her aside to sleep on the same bed, would need to wake her from a dream he hoped was of those cold nights under the quilt. He took his blanket and curled up on the floor.

When he woke at dawn, Maggie was already gone to her brother's factory, the bed left unmade, blankets twisted like withered husks.

The sky blazed pink when he got his sheep to pasture. Ren felt his fortune renewed, his to grasp like starlings fluttering overhead, and all he had to do was reach up and snatch one, wrap his fingers around spasming wings, squeeze a jittering heart. Today he'd implement active-shepherding techniques.

He started with Whitey, who had taken to munching a yellow patch of brittle grass. His lips puckered around a buried stone. Ren thwacked Whitey's rear with his staff, led him toward a greener area. As soon as Ren turned his back, Whitey moseyed back to the yellow patch to suck at the rock again. Ren tore fistfuls of green, pulled Whitey's mouth open, and jammed the bounty between his teeth. He kept cramming grass until his stained fingers cramped. His arms throbbed with the work, his back smarting. This was real work, and it felt good. Blood pulsed through his arms, thrummed in his ears.

The other sheep lingered in the greens, and Ren jogged from one to the next, shouting encouragement, jabbing his staff into the air, chanting, "Chew, chew chew!"

By noon, sweat soaked his frock. This was the work his father and grandfather had never dared. They would have shaken their wrinkled heads at the idea of innovation. He wondered if Maggie's brother was working this hard. He doubted it, doubted any workingman had ever worked so hard.

Ren began the next stage of active shepherding. He hooked the crook of his staff around the thick neck of his largest ram, Thor, and led him to Winona. It would be natural. His sheep just needed a little nudging. Today would be the day when the flock would flourish. The mood was perfect. Thor resisted, dragged his hooves, but Winona was nearing. Then came the clang of armor. Ren lost his grip on Thor.

The shoddy man-boy crested the rim of slate. He waved his sword at Ren until he lost track of his footing and tumbled down the hill. He rolled all the way to Whitey's feet, and Whitey licked the man-boy's arm.

"Hell of a sheep you have here," the man-boy said. "Cleaning my wounds, I see. And I didn't even have to call for a healer."

Ren thwacked Whitey away. He turned back toward the man-boy.

"When I eyed you, down there with your mighty-fighty lungs and your tough old staff, I said to myself, 'Thank Gurfay the Lucky Star Smasher above that my hero is here today,'" the man-boy said. "Just when you think it's over, war breaks out again, and I'm outnumbered like a shepherd to his herd, though it would have to be about three times as big as your herd."

A giant boulder crashed into the earth a dozen yards away from them. Ren looked up to the basin lip and saw the arm of a catapult. In moments, four more catapults appeared. A group of men bustled around each catapult, hoisted fresh boulders. Ren wondered if they sweated and strained as much as him doing active shepherding.

"You see, pops! Outnumbered. I tell you those big old stones make a man feel bitty. Might just be shit outta luck this battle."

Ren fingered the metal flute in his pocket, smiled at his secret. Another giant boulder thudded farther away. It must have taken a dozen men to lift just one boulder and a mule team dragging a cart for miles. A dozen wives and three dozen children left at home while they worked. The overhead was astronomical. And the effect was Ren and the man-boy could look up into the sky, watch these giant rocks blotting out the sun, and then move two feet to the left.

The boulders hailed down. More halberd- and sword-wielding soldiers ran down to clang swords and sidestep thunking boulders. Ren rushed through the field, gathering his sheep into a huddle around him so that they wouldn't be flattened. He thought he had all of them corralled into a tight circle, when he noticed, in the distance, Whitey lapping at a bloody, discarded breastplate. A shadow darkened Whitey's fur. Ren grappled for the flute. He pushed it to his lips and blew. It made a pathetic squeak just as a boulder swallowed Whitey.

Whitey's blood seeped through the grass, and that was all that was left of his oldest sheep. Ren blew on the flute again, and no one noticed. The men kept clanging, and the boulders kept dropping. He lifted Winona and clutched her to his chest. She was heavy in his arms. He didn't know if he could hold her until the battle finished, if it ever would.

The sun eventually burned red, then hid behind the basin lip. The catapults ceased, the clanging blades silenced, and the soldiers retreated up separate hills. Ren didn't see any bodies, any decisive victory. The only casualty was his lush grass, now acned with giant rocks.

"A battle to rattle the ancestors' graves!" The man-boy planted his foot on a boulder near Ren, puffed out his chest. "Guess that settles this fight for good. Until tomorrow, Shepherd."

Ren watched the man-boy sheathe his sword, crack his back, sigh with satisfaction. It all made Ren furious. "You certainly made enough noise to make your ancestors piss themselves laughing. What a joke."

"Now wait a goddamn minute. We're honor earning here. Fighting for our lives."

"How much honor, do you figure?" Ren waited for no answer. "What are you even doing here?"

"What aren't we doing? This is for everything: Land, religion, freedom from tyranny and ogres—once they're inevitably proven to exist. For the safety of my family, when I find the right buxom maiden, if you know what I mean." The man-boy waggled his hips. "But peace mostly, I suppose." He smiled, proud.

"So that's how it's done. That's how you make peace?"

"Listen, Shepherd, peacemaking takes time. I don't tell you how to do whatever you do with your sheep. My family's been doing this for generations."

"You must be so proud."

"I'm walking away, Shepherd," the man-boy flicked his sword at Ren, stepped backward, "so that I don't make peaceful pieces out of you, my old ally."

Ren snorted and watched the man-boy as he turned, as his shoulders drooped, as his sword dragged in the dirt, as the man-boy became a tiny speck on the basin lip and then disappeared again.

On his way home, Ren stopped by Tommy's again. A sign that read FOR LEASE THROUGH GOD blocked the cave mouth. Ren leaned over the sign and yelled, "I want a refund, Tommy. All thirds, Tommy. All of it back." Nothing stirred. Tommy was probably hiding, giggling, his hand over Franklin's muzzle. Or maybe Tommy and Franklin were dead, a pile of mixed human and sheep bones picked clean by bobcats. Ren flipped the coil of Maggie's hair around his index finger and peered into the black silence. He turned toward home. He hoped Maggie was still awake.

But the hovel was empty. No Maggie. No note. Just a mass of tangled blankets. She was likely working overtime. Ren could do that, too. Ren could do overtime even better, could become more of a ghost than Maggie. He could win a family, a future, alone, without Maggie, without anyone.

By moonlight, the half-buried boulders in his field looked like full bellies. Ren leaned into his staff, tired, dazed, but also focused, what his Grandpa Nork used to call the shepherd's drunk. That was a joy he'd forgotten, something that Tommy Two Bags couldn't teach. He watched his sheep disperse and maw at the night-blue grass.

When the man-boy appeared, Ren wasn't surprised. Ren slid behind a boulder and watched him stagger, lift a cask to his lips, drink. The man-boy spotted Thor and charged him. He smashed into his flanks and knocked the sheep over. Ren waited.

The man-boy gathered himself and stood. He lifted his foot over the ram's neck and then stopped. Ren heard him blubbering, one foot in the air, one on the ground, frozen like some kind of terrible dance. Ren was enjoying the show, the inanity of a soldier's solo performance. Only a shepherd could do it alone. Ren fisted Maggie's hair and then dropped it to the earth. He gripped the metal flute.

The man-boy unsheathed his stubby sword, raised it high over Thor's head. This was the man-boy's work. Ren understood. He required a partner for fighting. It didn't matter what the fighting produced. Production would never stop him. The man-boy would swing eternally at wisps in the dark.

Ren pitied the man-boy for his pointless labor, for its endless inevitability. And he hated that the man-boy required pity. Ren's grip on the flute tightened. He bolted forward, slammed into the man-boy. Ren stabbed his flute into the man-boy's thigh. It pierced the skin, and the man-boy screamed. Ren pushed harder, twisted the flute, made him howl. The howl morphed into a high-pitched bleating. Winona lay on her side a few boulders away. Ren jumped up and ran toward his ewe. She looked unharmed but continued to bleat madly. He ran his fingers through her coat, up her legs, down her neck, checking for the hot wetness of the wound the man-boy must have given her. As his fingers scoured her body, he glared at the man-boy, who was slinking behind one of the boulders.

Finally, his hands reached her tailhead. Under that, an unexpected roundness. A cold shock darted through his chest. There was the water bag, full and glistening. He hadn't noticed her heaviness when he'd clutched her against the catapults. He'd missed the signs for so long. But here it was—a lambing. This was what he'd been waiting for, and it had been here all along. Ren knelt beside her and massaged her coat, cooed into her ear.

A long time passed without the baaing he longed to hear. Just Winona's heavy panting. He wished it would be faster. The man-boy kept peeking from behind the boulder. One eye, half a dirty, childish face, and then he'd duck back into his ambush. He lurked in the darkness like a bobcat, like Tommy in his cave, waiting to pounce and collect. Ren wiped his hands against the inside of his robe. If he were closer to home, closer to Maggie, she could bring hot water and coffee. She could rub the ewe's hind legs. They would be a team working perfectly together.

But Ren was alone. Alone except for the man-boy, who leaned his head out from the boulder more boldly, his eyes wide and wild. Alone except for Papa Ander's ghost hand that had guided Ren through his first lambing decades ago, patient fingers that never knew rush. Ren bunched his fingers into a cone and pushed inside Winona. She struggled against him. The flesh around his wrist tensed. If she continued to fight, she'd never have this lamb, never have another. He longed for Maggie or Papa Ander or even Grandpa Nork to steady her.

The man-boy swayed above him against the stars. Ren was unable to defend his herd, his hand trapped, his fingers searching for wet lamb legs. The man-boy's thigh oozed blood. The blood trailed down his leg, dripped onto the grass. He dropped to his knees. The man-boy's hands wound around Winona's neck, roughly, in a way that made her jump. But then she calmed, and the man-boy eased his grip. The flesh around Ren's wrist loosened. He concentrated, felt the knotty angles of lamb elbows. He pushed the lamb deeper, until the elbows unlocked and the hooves lurched forward and out, and then the nose, the brow. He removed his hand, and the lamb followed.

It lay on his land, motionless, a wet pile of blood and moon. The man-boy gulped air. Winona licked at the still lamb. It baaed. It baaed impossibly, a little screech in the dead of the night. This lamb would become a ewe, which meant Ren could become a success. But Maggie would not be home when he returned carrying the new lamb. So he had this moment, these scratches of new breath, Winona and her lamb and the man-boy, who'd lost his sword somewhere. His silent armor gleamed in the moonlight alongside the wet lamb.

CONCH TONGUE

I GRAB UP MY MICROPHONE AND STROLL TO THE FRONT OF the tour bus. The clicking cameras turn from the shanties out the window and aim at me. I tear a giant smile into my face, and one camera blinks. Nothing much to see yet. I'm just the guide, another dark woman wearing a collar and name tag. They smatter sunblock on their husbands, on their wives. The bus smells like coconuts and sweat. A middle-aged couple in matching yellow Hawaiian shirts clutch their fanny packs and quiz each other with a laminated exchange-rate chart. When I get to the front, the youngest couple—twenty-year-old babies, honeymooning and pretty as a pair of polished stones—tug my shirt hem, whisper-ask where they can score the ganja. I spread that smile bigger, keep moving, snap on the mike.

It's time to sing. I swallow a breath and belt out Belafonte's "Day-O." The pasty legs uncross and start tapping. Now it's time to teach their version of our language. I chant: "No problem" and "Mon" and "Irie." They shoot it all back in pinched American syllables. We put it all together: "No problem, mon. We feelin' irie." The bus rings with hard Rs and squeaky vowels. Now they know everything, and all the pink lips smile. The cameras flash freely. I'm finally fit for a picture. I'm their Jamaica. They can print me on a four-by-six glossy and fold me into their wallets.

I've been running tour buses for three years now. Sunny Side Hotels promoted me from maid service when they heard me smooth talking the guests. They said they liked my voice, my people skills, but it's mostly because I'm a woman, youngish and half-pretty, short and skinny, one of the few dark-skinned workers the Americans don't fear. The guests ask me for everything: directions, drugs, towels, where to get the best jerk chicken, where to get one of those coconuts they can drink out of, where the jellyfish swim. I am the ambassador, and the money's good.

After the bus tours, I'm done for the day. But a few months ago, Busha Paul ordered me into his office. If we called him Busha to his face, he'd stomp around, lecture how lucky we have it, how free we are. He wants us to call him just Paul—just everybody's friend Paul.

Busha Paul assigned me the Trumans. Big-deal guests. Busha Paul already swept the maids into a tizzy for them, changing the royal-suite sheets three times over. I find the couple sweating through their khakis in line at the front desk. They look in their thirties, have hair so blond it looks like spiderwebs. I worry about their scalps sizzling. But I can't stop the sun.

I snatch them from the line, palm their bony shoulders, try to ease them toward the beach sunset. I'll handle check-in. Big-deal guests don't wait, don't sweat. Not with me. Everything's easy. Trust me.

Busha Paul says they own this online dating service Soul-Matrix. First time to Jamaica, but if things work out, they'll sell honeymoons at our hotel for their matched soul mates. Busha Paul says I'm to show them paradise, and if I do, if it all works out, the hotel will send their contractors to my house, fix it up perfect. A Sheetrocked room for my sons Desmond and Isaiah. Patch the leaky roof. Maybe an air conditioner for Grandmama Adina. No way I could ever fix it up on my own. A house that looks like a real house for my real family—that's a dream you don't want to wake from ever.

The government gave me this house of cracked mortar and frayed wires. It beats the shanties. No one is homeless in Jamaica. But no one's home is right. I'll never catch up to patch the leak dripping on Isaiah's forehead when he snores at night. Grandmama Adina's window is a gaping hole, and she wears a bug net that makes her look like a duppy bride. Not homeless, though. Oh no.

The Trumans hesitate to leave the check-in line, to leave their luggage with one of us dark strangers. So I slap leis over their necks, kiss their cheeks, send a pretty little waitress with big cups of piña coladas. They shuffle off to the beach, and I hurry to their room, double-check the bedding, direct the porter and shoo him out, fluff the hyacinths. A little blue-tailed skink hangs from their curtains, and I slap him down to the tiles. I kick at him, try to urge him to the door, but he scurries under the bed, disappears. And I say, "Okay, little man, you can stay. You watch over these big-deal sweeties from down there." I pray he'll stay hidden in the mattress springs.

When I get to the beach, the Trumans are wading, khakis rolled to their bony kneecaps. The sun boils purple into the ocean, and it feels good and strong against my cheeks, like Grandmama's hand before it got all shaky. I can even hear the ocean-dipped sun simmer. But I know suns don't simmer. That's not real. Simmer like a hiss, like a water snake. Not really a snake but just as bad. Uncle Alton's bald head rises from the ocean. His tobacco-stained, cotton-ball beard emerges dripping. He's whisper-hissing to the Trumans, waving them out, coaxing them with his pearly too-big dentures. The black iron fences surrounding the hotel compound keep out men like Alton—shell hawkers, ganja pushers, renegade hair braiders—but we can only keep the higglers so far. Nobody owns the ocean, so Alton's free to sell to anyone swimming his way.

Anyone but the Trumans. They aren't needing to meet sneaky-snaky old Uncle Alton.

I run to the beach, kicking fans of sand that fill my sneakers. The purple sun melts fiery on my neck. I stomp into the water, mud squishing in my shoes. I tap Mrs. Truman on the shoulder.

"Your room all ready, honey. Why don't you come inside to rest them tired traveling bones," I say, sweeter than syrup.

Uncle Alton's head dips back under the water, so just his yellow eyes watch me. The Trumans nod at each other and turn my way. I've saved them, won them. But Alton resurfaces, fist first, clutching a big conch shell.

"'Mericans! 'Im looka dis way see da magic shell I finding jus' fe you." Alton lifts the conch higher, as if he were a Sunny Side waiter serving filet mignon. "Pretty shell fe dis pretty white lady."

Mr. Truman wades toward Alton. His fingers skim the calm water, as if it were a bubble he might pop. Mrs. Truman sways next to me. Her plastic cup makes a popping sound.

"They aren't wanting your dirty old shells, Alton," I say. "They got a nice room waiting."

"Dis no dirty ol' shell." Alton flicks a tangle of seaweed off the conch. "Dis magic shell. Keep da secrets of Jamaica insi'. Whispa fe 'im de waves and san' and good people 'ere."

"Only thing that stinky shell keeping is a squirmy-germy mussel or something like that," I say. "They don't need your shell, unless they're wanting soup. And we have five-star chefs that can do much better for you, Mrs. Truman dear."

Mr. Truman wades to his waist, a couple of yards from Alton. He wrestles his T-shirt over his shoulders and tosses it to Mrs. Truman with a smile. The water sparkles off his bleach-white chest. "How much?"

"'Im wise one 'ere. Wise mon wan' da secrets." Alton dips the shell back under the ocean. "Ten dollas 'Merican and be yours."

Just when I'm certain the Trumans are smart enough not to have money on them, Mrs. Truman produces a fold of dollars from between her breasts. She peels off a ten-dollar bill and waves it high above her head, shouts, "He said ten American dollars."

By how proud and loud Mrs. Truman says the amount, I'm pretty sure these are the first words of Alton's she's understood. He's a dirty patois speaker, like Desmond's picking up, my oldest, though he's still just a pickney. Alton speaks low and fast like machine gun fire through a pillow. No guest understands that rumble or wants to hear it. But Mrs. Truman is all smiley and money waving now that she understood something. Price. Dollars. American cash. Everyone everywhere knows the words to that song.

Mr. Truman swishes to her and takes the bill from her fingertips, pecks her on the lips. "I bet I can get it for five. Want to see me haggle, baby?"

"Just give him ten," she says. "Look how much he needs the money. What would you do if our clients started haggling?"

"It's different commerce here. They expect it. The price he says isn't what he means."

She shakes her head until he clutches her chin and kisses her again. "Whatever you want, my love."

I'm soaking in sea brine, and all I can imagine is the pink mussel in the conch wrestling out like a swollen tongue in their luggage, sliming all over Mrs. Truman's lacy lingerie, Mr. Truman's satin ties. Then him storming into Busha Paul's office. My walls at home crumbling, a mouth erupting in the ceiling to dump water onto Isaiah's head.

"The lady says full price, my friend." Mr. Truman stretches the folded bill toward Alton, but Alton doesn't move. His woolly white beard bobs on the water.

"'Otel say no. You come fe Alton, so Babylon no come fe me."

Mr. Truman stands there smiling, gives the bill a little flap. We could wait all night, until the tide swoops over our noses. I want the Trumans sleeping in soft beds, and I want to read my boys a story before they fall asleep. I grab the ten bill from Mr. Truman and slosh out to Alton, up to my neck. I pass him the money, but before he gives me the shell, he holds my wrist, winks. I shake free and trudge back to the Trumans. Mrs. Truman puts the conch to her lips and blows. Nothing comes out but a squish. Mr. Truman pulls a wadded ten from his shorts and offers it to me. We don't take tips, can't take tips, and I tell him. He stares at the drenched uniform clinging to my body. I might as well be talking Alton's garbled tongue. Who don't want American money? I don't, but it's easier the other way. I take it, and finally the Trumans go to their room.

The next morning, no bus for us. The hotel rents a private car, shiny and black and not a single dent. I ride up front next to the driver—the Trumans, our precious cargo. They wear skintight short shorts and tank tops. I don't smell any coconut sunscreen, and I worry for their ghost-pale skin. We drive past the shanties, and I pour them drinks, sing them the tour-bus songs. They go zip-lining at Big Timba, and the trees and rivers blur under them like a pretty painting. I usually tell my tours about the ackee, grandpa tales about the Great River, but the Trumans push more sweaty dollar bills my way every time I start one of my speeches. I stop trying to talk.

The best part of the zip-line tour is the fences. Like the hotel, except these fences are taller, block out all the best parts of the forest. No ocean for the Altons to spill in from. Hundreds of acres of trees, and way up on the lines, the Trumans can't spot a single shanty. The holes in my roof would look like pinpricks from here.

After the zip line, the Trumans push dollars into the workers' palms. They swarm to unlatch the Trumans' lanyards, offer hands to guide them over rocks and back to the car. I hold the door open, and the Trumans try to push money at me. I pretend I don't see, don't say anything, but Mr. Truman stands there smiling until I take his bills.

On the way back to the hotel, the Trumans' eyelids dip heavy. Mr. Truman's head lolls onto Mrs. Truman's fire-kissed shoulder. He murmurs, "Paradise, baby." And I wish he'd say it again. Again and again to Busha Paul, and then maybe to my boys and Grandmama Adina. I'll fold his words, stash them in my pocket, and pull them out whenever the rain drip-drips through the roof. But there's no room in my pocket. It bulges with American dollars.

Busha Paul snatches me away from the Trumans when we return to Sunny Side. Busha Paul is a ball of muscle. He wears shorts, shows off his calves, which look like fists trying to punch through his skin. His mustache pulses when he asks about the Trumans, when he asks if everything is perfect.

"Mr. Truman says it's paradise," I tell him. I slip my fingers into my pockets and yank them away when the dollars crinkle.

"They met Uncle Alton." He stretches his right foot to his hip, balances on the other. "That's no good, girl. We want them with our people. Our best people."

"Which ones are ours?" The zip-line crew, the car driver, the girls selling polished conches at the gift shop instead of live ones from the sea? They're all wanting what Alton wants. Only difference is names scribbled on forms somewhere in Paul's filing cabinets.

He drops his right foot and stomps on the tile. "You know what I mean. The ones who sound right."

"I hear you, Paul."

"Good. Because we need the Trumans, which means you need the Trumans." His thumb and index finger press his mustache, and I wonder if the pink mussel that was in the conch has oozed out in the Trumans' hotel room yet. "Who are they with now?"

"Not me. I'm talking to you."

So Busha Paul pushes me out his door, into the lobby, and the Trumans are somewhere, pushing dollars into tired hands, forcing smiles on some bartender who's worrying about getting fired, trying to push the money back and explain the gratuity policy the Trumans refuse to hear.

I wander the bars, and no Trumans among all the sunburned shoulders and Hawaiian shirts. Not at the jerk hut and not along the beach. I scour the resort until the sun's almost gone, just a slit over the water, and Grandmama Adina will be fretting over some rice about now, my boys shoving through the front door from whatever trouble they've been into.

Out on the dock, I spot a mess of pink skin glowing against the dusk. Mr. Truman has stripped to a red Speedo and black water shoes, the Mrs. in a string bikini. Their near-white hair flaps in the night-promising breeze. Mr. Truman is bent over, smiling at something below him in the darkening water. Mrs. Truman sits on the dock, stretching her hand to the sea. On both of their backs, I see the outline of tank tops, where pink arms meet pale, untouched skin. Every time I see them, more of their skin has been claimed by our sun, but they always seem to stow a little whiteness away. I can't see what they watch in the water, though. I'm too far, and it's getting too dark to know anything. The moon's no help, just a straining sliver.

When I step onto the dock boards, I feel a punch in my belly. I sense him—Uncle Alton again, creep-creeping around too close to the beach. I should go back to Busha Paul, have him call the police, teach Alton a hard lesson. I tap across the dock, listen for the low spitting bullets of Alton's nocturnal sales pitch.

"Not jus' pretty beads, dese amagic. Made of dem dreams an' wants of all Jamaicans."

He's running through his romantic dream lines again. Every piece of rubbish Alton finds stores some secret power of Jamaica. Tonight, he's close enough to shore to stand, and over his bony shoulders his skeleton fingers grip and shake the necklaces around his neck. I'm so used to seeing only his head and his white beard that I'm surprised to see a body of twigs. So skinny, I wonder how he keeps going. His flicking tongue and giant dentures are the thickest parts of his body.

"Don't you love the way he talks, Toby," Mrs. Truman says. "We should have him get a drink with us."

"How about it, friend?" Mr. Truman says. He pulls a few dollars from inside his Speedo, and I'm surprised he can fit anything else in the fabric stretched tight over his crotch. "You look like you might want a drink and a bite to eat."

Alton scratches a long fingernail against his dentures. "Fe dem beads?"

"We want you to have a drink with us," Mr. Truman says again slowly, like he's talking to a toddler. "Maybe we'll find him a date, a soul mate. We're pretty good at that. Right, babe?"

"Me sell beads, but can nyam wid yu." Alton pulls the necklaces off his neck and holds them out to Mr. Truman. "No wan' bang-garang fe carry-go-bring-come lakka me."

"He wants to, right?" Mr. Truman looks my way, smiles. He aims the money at me. "You could join us, too. You're both our friends here now."

I take the money, just like Alton would. But my pockets are so stuffed it won't fit. "We're not really supposed to do that, sir, Mr. Truman." I wad the bill into a little ball about the size of one of the beads on Alton's necklace.

"Yu 'av' a twang dem get. Fe me dey sayin', 'No send, mon.'" Alton strips the necklaces from his neck, hands them over. "Tell dem ginnals me no mawga dawg. Tell dem I jus' sellin', not beggin'."

I hold the Trumans' money and Alton's necklaces. They're made of coffee beans and watermelon seeds needled through with nylon. I've seen thousands of these. I'm holding everything, but no one will get what they want. Maybe Alton, if I decide to toss this tiny ball of dollars, and then he'll take the Trumans' wadded crotch money and let the sea wash away their sweat as he wanders down the shoreline. He'll drag his bones for a mile, until he reaches land not owned by one hotel or another, where he can step to the sand and not worry about trespassing. If I could, I'd follow him to that nowhere beach. I'd slip into the night and forget about the Trumans waiting at the bar for me to speak without my twang. But I can't. I must join them while Busha Paul watches and the bartender pours me a drink that I won't drink. They'll talk and I won't talk about my boys and Adina. The Trumans don't need to know about Alton's callused feet or my drip-drip roof. And once they get home, open their luggage, the seeds and beans will have broken from the string. The conch's tongue will be all dried-up and dead.

ONE MORE FOR YOU

I MET FRANCO SIMMS IN THE SUMMER. EXTERIOR JOB—BOSS says I'm too messy to work on interiors, but I'm fast—a faded green two-story house on one of the hundred lakes that dot central Michigan, a beach-house rental we were painting with a new coat of green. Greener. Greenest. It was Franco's first day with us, but I found out later he'd been painting for years, decades, his whole life, came out his mother on a ladder with a brush in his hand the way the guy talked about it. I could tell from the start the guy was a talker.

It was July, right after the Fourth, fresh from a long weekend. Back to painting green, and tired, most of us hungover. Franco drove up in the morning, black licorice hanging from his mouth. He had short black hair, a bushy mustache, dark eyes, but everything else was white: pale skin, painter whites from shoes to shirt, all brand-new and spotless. The rest of the crew and me wore jeans and tank tops we'd shuck in a few hours. We were tan, pocked in green paint smears. Boss started Franco out with painting—no scraping, no spackling, no sanding, all the sweaty, dirty work done for him, right into a green cutting pot. Boss had told me I'd meet a real painter, a guy who could teach me how to swing a brush. But Franco was just another one of those old guys who thought they knew everything, set in their ways. I say, show me any old real painter, and I'll paint circles around him all day.

I got paired with him on the south side of the house. Franco and me on thirty-foot extension ladders. I pulled mine up first, right above a window to the peak. We always start from the top, left to right, just like reading. There's logic in that. While climbing my first rungs of the day, I smelled something like cherries burning. Franco had lit a Swisher Sweet. I watched him swing up his ladder to the right of mine. Bad form, to start from the right. He rattled up that ladder, barely using his hands for balance, smoking, his cutting pot clanking behind him, the black licorice traded for a brown cigar puffing in time with his steps. He settled in just below me with the angle of the eave, hung his pot on a rung, and mashed his brush inside.

"Paint a lot of exteriors?" He ashed his cigar into his cutting pot.

"Every day. Unless it's raining and until it starts snowing."

"But how long we talking?" A cherry cloud floated out of his question. "Few months, few years? You're a young guy. Can't be too long."

"My second summer." It didn't sound like much when I said it. But I knew the job, felt it in my callused palms, in my fingers that curled into a brush grip in my sleep.

"A little green to painting then."

"Yeah. I guess." I reached far away from him, mashing my brush to the soffit.

"Not too green, though. I see it wearing off. You've got a painter tan coming in, red in the neck and calves." He smiled, but I wasn't looking fully at him, only out the corner of an eye.

"This is a nice job. By the beach. Probably get a breeze. Maybe spot a honey in a two-piece." He had his eye on his work now. I checked to make sure he wasn't milking the job, watched the thin spot on the top of his head bob to his brushwork. "Always like the view from up here. Like home for me. How about you? Ladder work give you a little tingle in the undies?"

"I do what the boss says." I mashed my brush harder over Franco's head, hoped I'd nail that balding spot with a few green drips.

"So," he dipped his brush, slapped it against the inside of the pot, "I got a story for you." He kept slapping the brush, like a bird flapping its wings, natural, smooth, ready for takeoff. "I was working on this house once. Big Victorian monster, navy-blue body with red trim and yellow detail. Beautiful project. Had to use a dainty one-inch brush for all the yellow and red. Soft hands, you know. Laser eye. I was an hour into this trim around a spired add-on. Looked like a castle, this part. Like Rapunzel might throw down her hair at any moment. And I'm thinking this very thought about Rapunzel, working toward a window by my ladder, when the window creaks open. So I finish my section, go down, and slide my ladder right over top this open widow. I climb back up to my dainty detail work and can't help but take a peek inside. The sight I saw, goddamn, man. This beautiful Betty is inside lying on this bed, one of those things with lace canopies. And she's completely naked. She pulls up her knees and then spreads her legs, staring straight at me through those velvety thighs. She looked like a princess, a real Rapunzel, but with brown hair, maybe a little shorter. It's dark inside, but I can tell she's got bedroom eyes, not just because they're in a bedroom. I'm thinking, Just keep working, Franco. Ignore her. But she lifts an ankle and waves for me with these purple-painted toes. And now, hell, I can't think of anything else. The tiny brush in my hand won't move. I swing my leg around the ladder into the sill. Inside, I realize how sweaty I am, how my whites are filthy. But she don't care. She pulls me onto the bed. And I'm wrapped in satin sheets, never felt anything so soft. Fifteen minutes later, I'm back painting yellow, with a new appreciation for ladder work."

When Franco stopped talking, I woke up. That's what it felt like. I'd breezed through my section of siding, without remembering a single stroke. "So what happened next? What happened with your princess?"

"What happened is I painted that princess's tower perfect. Those lines were crisp. You couldn't see a wave or a holiday with binoculars. Totally unnecessary, but I couldn't help it. I had to do it right."

"But what about when her husband got home or her old man or whatever? What happened then?"

"Oh, him. He thought my work was perfect, too, even shook my hand."

I climbed down to move to a new section of green. A few steps down, I glanced into the window in front of me and my ladder. The sun glared hard off the pane. It made an opaque reflection of myself framed by aluminum rungs: skinny, shirtless, a five-day beard, red baseball cap spilling greasy curls. No princess, just me. "You know, Rapunzel was a fairy tale. Not real, not even close. Like perfect exterior painting," I said, descending.

"Shit, kid, you just need to spend more time on the ladder."

The top section of the house went quick. I was in rare form, sped up by the new old guy, like a lap horse. But Franco kept gaining. Every time I moved my ladder, his would clang up next to me in shorter and shorter intervals. We knocked out the top floor of the lake-facing south side in about two hours. And then we were on stepladders, then ground. Grass is a nice break after being on a ladder. Soft and even all around, no rungs pressing into the arcs of your soles. That's when I really whip through a job. And I was going fast, practically running with my brush on each row of siding: top to bottom, left to right, whole lengths at a time. Franco put down his brush and pot and picked up the nine-inch roller frame. He rolled out my rows, right on top of me, finishing all I started. He was killing me.

I'd taken the siding down to waist height, still flying, when I tripped. My cutting pot sailed out of my hands, plunked the ground, spilling paint onto the grass. Franco stood over me.

"That's irony for you." He lit another Swisher Sweet.

"What?" I braced myself, ready to take guff for my spill.

"Green paint on the green grass. Better yet, green painter spilling green paint on green grass."

"That's more like coincidence than irony. Or maybe a tongue twister."

He laughed in a loud shot. "Whatever you call it, it's not too bad. Don't even have to clean anything up."

I headed for the hose around the corner. I sprayed out the grass where I'd dumped the paint. The water made it foam light green. Otherwise, you couldn't tell.

"Imagine five gallons of bright-white enamel oozing down concrete stairs." Franco smoked, watching me spray, as if he thought my mistake meant break time. "I've done worse. That's for sure. You can't just hose off concrete. Too gritty. Have to scrub with wire brushes."

"I kicked over a full gallon of red stain last summer," I said. My toes curled secretly in my sneakers. "All over a brand-new wood deck."

"That had to hurt." Franco retrieved his roller, slopped it in the pan. "They give you some shit for that?"

I'd been trying to forget that story since it happened. "Not too bad, since we were staining it that color anyway. Actually, they all cheered right after it happened, slapped me on the back for thinking up a faster way to stain a deck. Sarcastic assholes." It felt different than I thought, telling it to Franco. It had felt like an open wound inside me, but right then, I could tell it had closed up. Maybe still a bit red, old and healed enough to be impressive though, some scar to show your friends.

I dumped more paint in my pot and got back to the siding. We were moving well again. My brush glided under each clap of siding. When I got to where Franco rolled, he'd hop out of the way like leapfrog.

"I got one for you." He didn't stop rolling. I didn't stop cutting. I knew what was coming. "We're driving down I-75 in this rusted-out pickup, this crew I used to work for, Painting Expressions. I'm in the front between the boss's oldest son and his youngest. We got a full bed filled with five-gallon buckets for this job south of Detroit. My forehead's practically touching the rearview, so all I'm seeing is backward. Through the mirror, I see a five go sliding off the bed, real smooth, like it might just keep floating. But then it hits the pavement, splatters everywhere in this huge streak of yellow. I turn to the oldest, the driver, Bruce or Bob or something, who doesn't even realize what just happened, and say, 'Shit! We just lost a bucket.' Before he registers what I'm telling him, another one goes, splashing yellow hell all over the road. Well, Bob or Bruce, he gets what's happening now. The road's pretty clear 'cause it's early, except for this semi bearing down on us. He's honking, flashing his headlights, as if we don't know. So what does Bob or Bruce do? He stomps the gas. He's thinking we gotta lose that semi before it reads our plate. And big surprise, another five shoots out, this time with some trajectory. It rails right into the grille of that semi, squashes like the fattest june bug you ever saw, full of yellow blood. Not just the grille, it's everywhere, plastering the lights, speckling the windshield, even flecking the side-view mirrors. I swear I saw a splotch on the driver's arm. Now that's some painting expression. He pulls onto the shoulder. We take the next exit and stick to the back roads."

Franco rolled out the last section just as he finished his story. I was standing there, just watching him. I couldn't remember if I'd even cut that last section.

"What about the semi? Bob or Bruce, he get busted?"

"Never heard a peep about it." He tossed the roller into the pan, plucked a piece of licorice from his front pocket, and snapped his teeth around it. "All they had to worry about was stretching materials since they were now fifteen gallons down."

It seemed like there had to be more. I wanted some kind of ending where Bob or Bruce faced the consequences. Some fistfight between burly truck driver and wiry painter. Or the boss's son getting fired by his dad. I wanted Franco's stories to be more than just a way to kill time. Where was the moral, the meaning?

"Did they stretch it?" I said.

"Hell no!" Franco smiled at me. "They wasted half a day waiting for another order at the paint store."

Maybe it was a lesson about patience or wastefulness. I guess it didn't matter so much, because he could spin a fine story. He'd topped mine about the stain. But I had more.

"Last year, we were painting a cookie cutter in one of those new subdivisions," I said. "You know the type, where every house matches, as if God just dropped them right into perfect little squares of green sod. Perfectly spaced. Shiny and new. Like big boxy babies from the same litter." I cleared my throat. Wanted to make sure every word was crisp. "The one we were working on looked the same, too. But the homeowners wanted to make it stand out with a new color. Some kind of beige to Brunswick Blue or Breakwater Blue or some fancy blue. Who names those paint colors anyway? That's gotta be the easiest job in the world." I looked over at Franco.

He was nodding his head. "I hear you. Dream job, inventing colors."

"Yeah, yeah. So this house, it wasn't like it needed a paint job. Just some people got so much money they can afford to get sick of looking at the same color. The first day, we had the whole front side painted. But the homeowner, the husband, he gets home from work, steps out of his silver BMW, looks at our work, and runs inside. He runs back out with a paint swatch, slaps it against what we'd painted, and starts stomping his feet. He says we painted it the wrong color. We're off by two and a half shades. It's our fault even though we don't tint the colors. All the work we did that day, all for nothing. We have to reorder the right paint. Boss is pissed. He has to eat it, pay for all that extra wrong-colored blue. But he doesn't want it. No room to store it and hope someone wants that exact color in the future. So he has me dump it down the sewer grate, like thirty gallons."

Franco cut in, "And now Michigan's drinking water is bluer than ever, thanks to you." Franco stretched his arm, pointed his roller at the lake. "That's boss man for you. They leave the dirty work for their guys. Clean hands to sign the checks with."

"No. That's not it." My skin felt hot, burning inside my tan. "I like my boss okay. It wasn't his fault."

"But those rich homeowners, they're a picky bunch."

"Not them either. It's just," I took a deep breath, "all that blue. Wasted, you know?"

He sucked up the last bit of licorice dangling from his mouth. "When do you guys eat?"

My story had fallen apart. I couldn't get my hands around it. The shape of that blue. If Franco hadn't kept interrupting, I could've found the point to the whole thing. It was right there, like that last dull section of siding surrounded by a fresh coat.

After lunch, I had a chance to look over our work. His side of the house was full of holidays, the underside of his boards all pale green where his brush had skipped. That was how he'd gone so fast, been able to keep up with me. If the boss had seen his work, Franco would've been on his way home. But quality control wasn't my job. I was just a brush swinger.

We moved to the next side, where a pea-stone driveway skirted the house. Franco and I stayed paired up. This time, I let him set his ladder first, and he chose the second-story peak. After he climbed a few rungs, puffing a fresh Swisher Sweet, I set up on the far left side. We had some distance between us, twenty feet or so, our work no longer overlapping. Now I knew Franco wasn't the painter he said he was, but I needed to see what I had, prove I could beat even a cheater.

Over lunch, the bristles of my brush had hardened. I'd left my brush in the pot, in shade, even covered it with a rag, but nothing could hide from the cooking noon sun. I stood at the top of my ladder, picking globs out of the bristles, while Franco eased into an early lead.

"It's a hot one," he said. "But not the hottest I've seen. I spent a couple of years in the Keys, painting hotel fronts. Now that was hot. Your brush could brick up in minutes."

Green paint covered my fingertips, but at least my bristles moved again. "The Keys, huh?" I let him tell me another one. Talking would slow him up.

"Yep."

"What was that like?"

"Not much to say about that. People think it's this magical place. And maybe it was once. Hemingway house, six-toed cats, every reel taut with a marlin, beaches, palm trees, all that shit. I saw hotels. All those bright colors, you'd think they'd be fun to paint. After a while, they made me sick. The whole place did. Didn't see my wife for months at a time. She was way back home. And when I got back, she wasn't. But there's not much story in that."

He stopped brushing to squeeze out the cherry of his Swisher Sweet between his fingers and pocket the butt. The brown and burnt tobacco shavings sprinkled to the ground. He dug in his front pocket for another piece of licorice. All this gave me time to get farther ahead with my siding. The mention of his wife gave him reason to pause, to refill his mouth with something else, slow him up.

"What was your old lady like?"

He turned and squinted at the sun, his face all crinkled. "Definitely no fairy tale. She was a hard woman, pushy, hot tempered, with a light mustache she refused to do anything about, and she was always too busy with something else to be busy with me. But goddamn, could she cook. The smell of her kitchen was home for me. I remember one time I was working on painting the inside of this grocery store. We were spraying white dryfall into the steel girders. Ever used it? Awful stuff. It's supposed to be easy to clean up, the overspray drying into flakes before it hits ground. It's weird, changing from mist to crud in midair. That place looked like a blizzard once a few sprayers were running. I wore a respirator, but it kept getting clogged up. I'd take off my mask and bang out the filters every ten minutes. By the end of the day, all I could taste was oil in the back of my throat. White covered me from head to toe. Like a snowman or a ghost. Pure white. When I got home, Aggie, that was her name, swung at me with this huge oak crucifix we kept by the front door. Probably thought I was her grandpa returning from the grave. I almost broke my arm stopping her swing. She could defend herself. It made me proud. Bruised, too. Anyway, she'd cooked up the meanest batch of enchiladas I ever smelled. I like mine hot, and these ones burned my nose from the doorway. I didn't even clean up. Sat my ghostly self down at the kitchen table and ate right out of the pan. All I tasted was oil in the back of my throat, though. Aggie's hottest sauce couldn't burn through. That was the only lie I ever told, telling her they were delicious. That day, I felt like a ghost. Couldn't find my way home."

He stopped painting and wiped his forehead with his shirt. I was going to ask more about her—why she left. I was waiting for him to stumble over his story as I had, trying to make sense of that blue paint. But Franco's ladder interrupted. It made a grinding noise on the pea stone below us, kicking out, slipping down two claps of siding with a thunk, thunk. Franco's body jerked, and he grabbed the eave of the roof. Time froze. We stared at each other, and he made this face to me that said, What's next?

The ladder kicked out the rest of the way. It slid down a few more claps, shuddered, and slammed sideways against the ground. I watched it fall, couldn't help myself. When I looked back up, Franco dangled from the peak by one hand. In his other hand, he held his cutting pot and brush. I shot down my ladder, glancing up every few rungs, and there was Franco, legs dangling, his face turned toward the siding. I got to the ground and swung my ladder over. But before I got it under him, I looked up and stopped—Franco had put his brush to the siding, guiding it along while he balanced his pot in his hooked pinky finger. That was a sight, a ladderless painter, as if he were floating. He never quit painting, and I guess that was how I took him by surprise. I'd meant to get my ladder just under him so he could step down, be saved. But I moved too quick, miscalculated, skimmed the ladder against his legs. He flinched when the aluminum kissed his calves. He lost his grip, became airborne. It might not have been too bad a fall if not for the ladder I placed. His foot caught in the rungs, somersaulting his body, rotating him downward then rightward again, flipping, the green paint from his pot showering around me. He landed in the pea stone feetfirst, like some kind of acrobatic stunt landing. But then he crumpled, fell to his knees.

I stared at the top of his head. The balding spot glared from the sun shooting through the breaks in the oak leaves. The shiny spot on his head pointed up. I followed its direction to the siding we'd been working on. This side, unlike the other, was perfect. Not a single faded patch on his half or mine. His earlier work would have gotten him fired. But now this! And his grace, hanging by the eave. I would've chucked my pot and held on with both hands. Who wouldn't?

Later, my boss drove him to the hospital but didn't stick around. He left Franco in the emergency room. I never heard about him again. I never asked. But I'll always remember him floating. How his body tumbled against the rungs. His perfect landing, the way his knees caved. How he didn't make a sound after it happened, just braced his hands against his thighs until we carried him to the work truck. The last patch he'd painted was still shiny, still wet, but drying in blotches. Maybe I imagined the shoddy work he'd done earlier. Maybe he'd just noticed me paying attention, knew he couldn't get away with bullshitting me. But then that meant he had it in him all along. And how could I compete with a real painter with real stories? No matter now. This story's mine and Franco's. And I'm the one who gets to tell it.

STRONG AS PAPER MEN

THE BOYS WEAVED THROUGH THE DARKNESS, HIKED THROUGH demolition rubble to the mounded base of the abandoned powerhouse, where they tilted their necks to the tallest walls in the neighborhood. Almost every window was broken, but Topper and Sloan threw stones anyway, just to hear them plunk and echo inside the cavernous tower. They both loved the top of the rubble hill where the powerhouse stood, towering high enough that they could see both of their fathers' houses, watch cop cars creep in and out of alleys, see whose lights were on at midnight. The liquor store's yellow neon sign glowed, a nightlight for winos. Rusted slides and playground structures spidered the elementary school, its cracked red bricks. Up at the powerhouse, they felt different than their neighbors and their daytime selves. They were free from all of it, escaped from their mothers past midnight in summer.

The city of Kalamazoo had demolished most of the old paper mill, all but the powerhouse, which loomed four stories over the boys' neighborhood of two-story houses, peeling paint and sagging porches. Jagged concrete slabs and boulders littered the vacant field surrounding the lone building. Topper imagined exploring the powerhouse like breaking in and out of Alcatraz. He wondered if Alcatraz was anything like the jail his older brother spent last year in. Sloan—the younger of the two by four months, not yet fifteen—thought of Kilimanjaro, the harrowing rock inclines Mr. Bendele showed him pictures of at school. A challenge, a quest, only halfway completed at the summit.

Sloan heaved a hunk of concrete the size of his head at the powerhouse. It thunked against the first-floor wall, landed with a dead smack against the ground.

"You trying to take the whole place down in one throw?" Topper laughed, slapping his fingers against his thighs.

"I'm taking a stand." Sloan rubbed the sting out of his palms, much smaller, but more callused than Topper's long hands and bony knuckles.

"You against the world." Topper threw another stone high up to the third story. He just missed one of the few panes still holding glass.

"Hell yeah, man."

"That shit never happens. People get sick of trying. Give up."

"Not me," Sloan said, and it was mostly true. He did all his homework, finished every book and filled Topper in on endings, and most middles, and reminded him how they started. He'd completed three World War II battleship model kits, used every piece, even hand painted waving officers in the tiny windows. He mowed the cramped lawns in the neighborhood and weed whacked all the tight spots. But there was that father-son bowling team he quit. And then, of course, the ant farm. He'd found the shiny, black corpses piled on the topsoil, an ant cemetery. Even the last survivor must have limped over and collapsed on the paling thoraxes of its neighbors.

"Hey, sometimes quitting is good. Like me. I'm quitting smoking." Topper pulled out the newest pack of Virginia Slims he'd stolen from his mom's carton. "Starting next week."

Topper had smoked for two months and felt like he was getting an addiction. Only adults had addictions. He probably wouldn't quit. He'd quit quitting. Topper was an excellent quitter. He'd had three jobs already—babysitting for the Hoskas, painting houses for his cousin in the summer, sweeping the stockroom at his uncle's store—and quit every single one with grace and promptness. Why string anyone along if the mood wasn't right? Better to break off clean. He'd dated five of the best-looking girls in the ninth grade and one in the tenth, and he ended each relationship with a long-stemmed rose and a cursive note saying how he'd always cherish their love. The world was full of opportunities.

"Smoke up, man." Topper slid another smoke out of the pack and offered it to his friend.

"Not out here where everyone can see," Sloan said.

"Who cares?" Topper put both cigarettes in his mouth and lit them. "No one's watching."

"Never know. I don't want my parents finding out I smoke."

"You'll have to grow up someday, dude." Topper walked away from Sloan into the shadows of the powerhouse, smoking two cigarettes at once. His face disappeared, but the two cherries glowed through the darkness like a set of wild eyes.

Across Belford Street, Millie Bliss rummaged through her dead husband's footlocker and found his binoculars so she could watch the boys close-up. She pressed the dusty eyecups against her skin and knelt at her attic window. The powerhouse rocketed over the crooked pine treetops and roofs with flaking-scab shingles. Even without the bustle of industry, the powerhouse still had strength, exclaimed to the neighborhood, *I made you*, even if no one listened.

She saw Topper fade into the powerhouse's shadow. Before it swallowed him, she recalled his smooth black skin, his tall frame, his quick-talking charm. She'd watched him and his brother grow up. They were both beautiful boys bound for trouble, always laughing, sprinting down sidewalks as children, and then skipping school and strutting down the grassy median. She spotted Sloan next. He kicked up a gravel cloud and then followed, disappearing into the same shadow. He wasn't near as good-looking with his acne and mixed lighter skin, but he made up for it with hard work, mowing her lawn every Saturday. And he was smart, his name always printed in the newspaper's honor roll.

They were small silhouettes next to the building, and then they were gone, pulled into its mystery. She hoped for bright futures for these boys with chances, said prayers every night to bless them.

She caught the boys last month when investigating suspicious sounds at the powerhouse. She thought drug addicts or Jehovah's Witnesses might be planning to squat the abandoned lot. Her flashlight had flooded the wall of broken windows, the mouth of shattered gaps. But the boys were quick and evaded her light. She waited until two in the morning for the boys to leave, hiding herself behind a slab of concrete with jutting rebar ribs. They passed close enough for her to recognize their faces. Not junkies. Not solicitors of religious crank. Just kids.

Since that night, she'd been leaving gifts from her dead husband's footlocker for the boys in their clubhouse: her husband's jackknife, a flask half-filled with rum, an illustrated copy of *Huck Finn*, a 1945 military-issued map of New Delhi, a taxidermy ferret, the month of July torn from a pinup calendar featuring a cowgirl in hat and chaps hugging her breasts. Every few nights, she'd chuck an item through the windows of the old factory building and imagine the wonder the boys would have in finding these artifacts. They shared these secrets. But the boys wouldn't know it was her. They'd think these items were left behind. They were archaeologists. Historians. Discovering the culture of this neighborhood, even if it was inaccurate. They had to have interest, or it would be forgotten.

Someone had to want to know.

Sixty years ago, when Millie was the age of the boys, a neighborhood barely existed here. The whole area spouted smoke stacks. Factories for everything: Kellogg's cereal city, yellow Checker taxicabs, Upjohn pharmaceuticals, Gibson guitars, and paper and paper and paper. Paper mills consumed the city. Her father had built them a house next to his job at the mill, making them one of the first black families of the factory village. Boilers rumbled through the streets, engines growled. Men in overalls grunted, laughed, while coal burned and brought the biting odors of chlorine and sulfur. She lived in that house all her life. Her father left it to her husband after her husband returned from the war. But the neighborhood grew quieter every year. So few of the factories remained. By the time her husband died, the city was skeletal architecture, phantom industry. And the mill buildings, too, slowly collapsed under snow, orange fangs of arson, crunched in backhoe jaws. Soon only the powerhouse remained. Then the lights went out. Then nothing but a shell. With the treasures she left the boys, she might teach them, help them stumble onto the strength of the paper-mill men.

She rose from her knees and clicked off her record player spinning Jimmy Rushing. She pulled a chair to the window to sit in darkness and silence, waiting for the boys of this new neighborhood to learn manhood.

Topper jumped up and grabbed onto the windowsill above him, a low window they'd been using for weeks to sneak inside. Sloan heaved Topper's sneakers from below, and Topper tumbled in. There was a barricaded door to the powerhouse, but if they kicked it down, others would know what they knew, that this was a place for explorers, and they'd lose their island tower.

"Nearly broke my leg, tough guy," Topper said, yanking Sloan up into the building.

The streetlights projected a grid of broken windows against behemoth boilers inside. Everything was bigger in the factory. The boilers stretched upward into the highest floors toward an endless ceiling. Massive bundles of piping chased the catwalks. Topper scooped a handful of gravel from the concrete floor and hurled it against one of the boilers. A shower of pelting gravel erupted into the high ceiling and echoed thunder back to the boys. It sounded great from outside, but inside was even better. Sprinkle to downpour. Pebbles to boulders.

Alex stirred from a daze. She'd been crashed out on the top floor, but the thunder below brought her back, budged her iron eyelids open.

She didn't hear the initial noise. She felt it from under, rumbling her bones. The feeling of bones again. Bones humming, resonating, in reaction to something she had witnessed in half sleep, like the sense of a stranger in a dark room. She tried to yell but couldn't open her mouth, and the sound pushed through her teeth in a growl. She stomped the bones of her foot against the floor.

She hated being reminded of bones, of body. She wanted to slam her fist against the plywood floor. The thought stung her knuckles. The warmth of imaginary bleeding. She conceded to the stranger somewhere—ghosts in a squat, ghosts everywhere you go. There was nothing she could do about that.

She was too stoned, had been shooting more heroin, because she'd been getting more money. Down below, in the giant room with the boilers and sprawling pipes like a thousand copper snakes, just after sunset, treasures appeared. She kept finding things, good things, that she could sell. Knives, silver, old calendars—who knew? The remnants of paper making. The old mill, such an odd place. And pawnshops paid money for these things, which meant less money she had to earn by pleasing men, her head shoved down by sweaty hands in the front seats of strange cars. Every day, she marveled at what she'd find, what someone would pay for something other than drugs or sex. The treasures of ghosts appeared every few nights. And when she'd crawl down from the crow's nest at the top of the powerhouse, down the rusted iron ladder to find treasure, she'd get fucked up. A short walk to Hayes Park to buy as much as she could and then crawl back to her fortress at the top with the big windows, where she hunted stars.

Only there, hovering over streetlights and city halo, Alex was sure she'd find them. She had to climb, despite her plum-bruised forearms, to find a place farthest from light. This area of the city was easy to find drugs in. But she'd found more. Her white skin stuck out in this neighborhood, and the darkest skies made for the brightest stars. She felt special, rare, like a diamond, sparkling.

Time taught her how dully she glowed, though, how stars wouldn't shine like she'd hoped. She couldn't find Cassiopeia,

Orion, Virgo, just disembodied specks. She could never go far enough for stars. The city made them bland. Washed out the dark. Blended and blurred the intricate millions. So she settled for moon burn paling her motionless skin. Instead of finding herself against the dark, maybe she would fade into the powerhouse. She was ready to give up, blink out. She was high, and that was enough.

"Did you hear something?" Sloan asked.

Topper lit a fresh cigarette off the cherry of the one he'd been smoking. "You're paranoid, man." He exhaled a curl of smoke into a square of streetlight. The smoke looked like a dragon devouring its own tail. "Nobody goes inside this place. Just us."

"No. I heard something above." He pointed into the endless ceiling. "Up there."

"Hear this." Topper grabbed a damp piece of lumber from the floor and swung it against a boiler. "I'm mad as hell, and I'm gonna break some shit."

This time, they both heard a muffled growl from above, and they held their breaths. They slipped into a shadow space between two giant boilers. Topper stepped out first, chuckling to cover the sound of his heavy breaths.

"You think someone's here?" Sloan asked in a low voice.

"If there is, I want to know how they got up there and why *we* haven't figured it out yet."

"Let's get out of here."

"No way." Topper tilted his neck back, allowing his vision to swim in the darkness above. "We gotta find out."

"It's nothing that matters," Sloan said.

"It's something." He bolted up the nearest catwalk, his shoes clanking against the grates. "Let me know when you grow a pair."

"I got a pair. I got a brain, too, and it's telling me to go home." Sloan stepped out of the shadows but still spoke low. "Anyway, I got lawns to mow tomorrow." He headed for the window they used as an entrance, soon to be his exit.

By the time Sloan had his leg over the sill, Topper had spotted a ray of light whiter than the yellowed streetlights that gridded the inside walls. Following this light, he spotted rungs like train tracks against the wall, leading from the catwalk to the ceiling. Topper knew the maze of almost every pipe and catwalk, except for one path—from outside a crow's nest set at the top of the powerhouse. The boys had never discovered the route from inside. Now he knew why: the first few rungs had been demolished, camouflaging the path. The city didn't want them up there. Too close to the top. But like much of their efforts to safeguard the neighborhood, the few missing rungs wouldn't stop anyone willing. Topper had enough desire and the luck to find it. Everything aligned just right, the moon strong and bright outside to reveal the path, a growl like a beacon to lure him. "We must be blind to have missed this. It's the fucking top of the neighborhood."

Sloan paused, looked back toward his friend. He knew he'd have to go, make sure Topper didn't do something stupid. The greatest heights meant the greatest powers, the greatest dangers. And it meant knowing every place of the powerhouse. He had no choice. It was finishing in a way. He imagined his shoes crunching the stones on top of Kilimanjaro.

"Where are you?"

"See this?" Topper flicked his lighter.

Far above, Topper's sparks lit up the room. Sloan followed the flashes up and around the catwalks until he found his friend already scaling the ladder they'd never found, always missed. Topper easily jumped the gap in the ladder and scrambled up the wall. The sound of his sneakers climbing the metal rungs made a *ting ting*.

This time, Alex knew someone was there. The tapping of metal, the head sprouting from the floor. Then his shoulders. Here he comes. They found her. Ghost. Then two ghosts. Ghosts looking like boys with moonstruck wide eyes and hair cropped close to shiny heads. Factory workers from a previous time, must be, returned to recover the things she'd stolen and sold. She thought they'd be older. She'd been waiting for them. They'd absorb her in place of their treasures, suck her into their black-sky history.

That could be, she supposed. There could have been child labor, like Blake's little chimney sweeps. Fingers lost in pulp presses, ears dulled by mechanical roar, skin sliced by endless paper cuts. She smelled the grease and paper and blood. Oily red iron and pulp-caked steel. If it's ghost children, so be it. They have the right to haunt just like any other. They worked hard to die.

One stared down at her, wearing the crumpled brow of an older man. He was asking something of her. She felt her ether evaporating into a cloud, yellow, curling, pulling toward him. Her body was collapsing into human slush, puddle flesh. It was warm, quiet, soft, dark. Easy to go. She closed her eyes.

"Think she's dead?" Sloan asked his friend.

Topper prodded her thigh with the toe of his shoe. Nothing. He kicked her softly. Her leg twitched. "Nope. Fucked up is what she is."

Sloan bent close to her and listened for breathing. "Are you sure?" He could smell her hair. Like dry dirt. Like the crushed concrete that circled the lot outside the powerhouse, the smell of their secret freedom.

"She's not dead, but she sure as hell ain't here." Topper picked up one of her arms and waved to Sloan with it, the limp fingers flopping hello. "She's on Jupiter, man. Maybe fucking Pluto."

"That's not cool. She might be in trouble." He grabbed her limp hand from Topper, rested it gently in her lap. "We should call an ambulance or something. What if she's ODing?"

"Then a dopehead dies. You think they give a shit about that, man? She's hopping planets to us, but she's definitely dead to them."

"Who's them?"

"You're such a dolt." Topper blew a cloud of smoke into her face. "The Man, man. The Man don't care about her. The Man don't care about us."

Sloan had heard this sermon before. Topper picked it up from his brother, who hated the world. Topper was crazy about his brother, and since his brother hated the world, Topper did too, found more reasons every day. It was stupid. The world was too big to blur all together.

"Well, I'm not the Man, and I do care," Sloan said.

"You certainly are not a man, my friend, but that's beside the point."

He ignored the insult. Sloan didn't need to prove himself with a lip of soft hairs like the ones Topper grew on his lip, trying to look like his brother—the ultimate man, the righteous rebel. Sloan's actions would make him a man. Just like Teddy Roosevelt, whom Mr. Bendele had taught him about. A rough-riding motherfucker who could still be a teddy bear.

Sloan slid his hand under her legs, his arm rubbing against her buttocks. It made him tingle, and he felt warmth, wet. She was pissing on him. But heroes aren't stopped by a little piss. He reached his other arm behind her neck, bent his knees, his face close to hers. Her jaw and lips were sunk, and it made her look like she was puckering. She was kind of pretty. A crooked nose in a pleasing way, short bangs that curled into her eyes. The way her eyes hid under those bangs intrigued him. Maybe she'd see him someday. Thank him. He struggled to stand with her in his arms.

"What the fuck?" Topper laughed. "Here goes the tough guy again."

His friend tottered for a few steps with the weight of a woman in his arms. Topper thought she looked like a squashed spider, thin, lifeless limbs dangling. There was no way Sloan could go anywhere with this except into trouble. Topper's aunt smoked meth. She'd sit on the couch for hours, disassembling alarm clocks and television remotes in a trance. She had no understanding of the precise arrangement of circuit boards and wires and plastic casings, but she carried on, taking everything apart and leaving electronic guts everywhere she went. Her face fell apart within months. She stopped being a woman. Stopped being a person. More like the jumbled mess of dissected electronics than any person. When she finally got busted, Topper's dad had come to her defense, pleading with the cops. His silhouette became blank and black against the backdrop of blue and red lights flooding the street. They made his dad lie face down on the sidewalk, hands behind his head, while Topper and his brother watched from the porch. His aunt, a waste, had done this to his father. Kalamazoo was full of junkies. They were all just waiting to leech, suck the life out of people. And now Sloan carried one like she was Sleeping Beauty.

Sloan wasn't strong enough to do it alone, though, so Topper grabbed on to the legs of the woman for his friend's sake. Her middle slumped toward the floor. They toted her like this to the ladder.

"Okay, genius, how do we get her down?" Topper asked.

"I don't know." Sloan peered through the access hole to the catwalk ten feet down and the continuing blackness below. "We lower her, like with a rope or something."

"Ah shit, I happened to pick this day to leave my utility belt at home." He adjusted the weight of her legs higher up into his arms. "Where you gonna get rope?"

"She's pretty light. It's not like we need heavy-duty rope or anything."

"Your ideas suck, man." Topper spit his cigarette down the hole. The orange cherry bounced through the catwalk into the black below. "This is going to suck."

Rough plywood pushed against Alex's lower back, her bare forearms, the back of her head. The two child ghosts stood above her. They slipped off their shirts like skins of white. Their chests reflected moon, waning and waxing pectoral as their bodies shifted. Maybe they weren't ghosts. Instead of from the powerhouse below, maybe from above, from the sky she watched all nights, let burn into her own skin. They removed their pants, and their white shorts were the brightest sight she had ever seen. Like one of those constellations she could never find. She'd forgotten how amazing it was to put the pieces together. For specks to manifest heroes.

"It still won't be enough," they said. They looked down at her, summing up the variables, calculating her deflated, gelatinous body. What else did they want? How could she be enough? "We'll need hers, too."

Something of hers. They wanted to take it. Excavate. Salvage for parts. She wouldn't stop them. She'd stolen their history, sold it to the pawnshop. She would compensate with body.

"You do it." One knelt near her head. She clenched her eyes tight. Her T-shirt lifted over her stomach, her breasts, bunching in the back. Fingers slid between her skin and jeans, fiddling with her buttons. Over her hips, knees, feet. Denim and cotton ebb. Everything soft gone. Every part of her cold. How could she resist the sky coming to her tonight? She could be Leda to see the sky so close, in the form of ghost children.

"Congratulations on getting your first girl naked," Topper said.

"Fuck you. You can't take anything seriously." Sloan worked alone, knotting the woman's clothes they'd removed to their own. He didn't want Topper to notice the piss on her jeans. He'd make a big deal, give up. Sloan needed him. He was nervous around her. Topper never was. "She's still got on underwear."

"All the same, credit where credit's due," Topper said. "This is completely fucking nuts, by the way."

Sloan wrapped the legs of his pants under the woman's arms, crafting a makeshift harness. He tugged at the knots.

"Now what?" Topper asked.

"I think we're ready to lower her."

"Down the fucking rabbit hole." Topper tugged the woman's legs toward the access hole where the ladder descended to the catwalk.

"Slow down." Sloan waddled behind, struggling to keep her head from skidding across the floor. "Stop. Stop."

"What, man?"

"You can't just drop her down. We have to do it right."

"Taking your time. You're such a romantic."

Under Sloan's direction, Topper wound the rope of clothes around his back, bracing himself. Sloan lowered her body, an inch at a time, through the hole. The rope jerked as she slipped over the brim, and Topper struggled to ignore the sting of the noose around his back. Sloan wrapped the rope around one arm and slowly let the knots strain through his palms. There went Topper's black T-shirt, then Sloan's tan cargo pants, the woman's piss-soaked jeans. These knots strong enough to save a woman ground into the boys' skin, forcing the same welts to surface on both of their bodies.

Alex began a slow spin. She was sinking now. Lowering into a new place. Darkness, then squares of yellow light came and went and came again. Her shoulders felt heavy, armpits pulled and stretched. Legs lost already in an eddy of shadows. She couldn't feel them. Would she ever find her legs again? Somewhere at the bottom? Hell's a shoe closet full of toes and tendons and achilles heels. Body parts strewn about. Impossible to sort. You are stumps. You are pieces. She realized now she could not face dismemberment, being salvaged for parts, becoming a part of these ghosts' world. She raised her arms, attempting to swim the air, birth herself upward from gravity. But she couldn't break the knots they'd tied.

They were getting close now. If Sloan's palms held out, if Topper's torso didn't split, she'd land on the catwalk soon. And after that, Sloan thought, they would save a woman's life. But in front of them, the fabric hissed, the sounds of failure. Sloan gripped tighter, slowed the rope's drop. He could see it, the woman's T-shirt, caught on a shard of metal over the access hole. The fabric was too weak; the powerhouse's metal bones, too sharp. He tried to go faster now, yelled to Topper to let out more line. The rope burned harder into their skin, dragged them across the plywood. The rope snapped. Below, they heard the woman's body clang against the catwalk.

They watched her through their rip in the universe, the one she'd fallen through. Their words bled down on her.

"That was the dumbest fucking idea."

Alex could feel them. Legs again. Impossible discovery. Throbbing, pumping, but nothing in her left foot. No toes. Swept away.

"Are you still alive, lady?"

"What makes you think she'll answer you now?"

Alive? No way to tell. Hell hurt, right? She tried to move a hand to pinch herself. Or was that only for dreams? Her fingers lifted like boulders. She gave up, left them wherever they were.

"Sloan, why do I smell like piss?"

She smelled it, too. Those distant, hollow voices above commanded her senses.

"What do you think we should do now?"

"Hey, you're the man with the plan," one of them said. "I still smell piss."

She smelled it more acutely now. Ammonia pangs. What color would clouds of ammonia be in a nebula? Great curling fangs of blue or yellow? Torrent gaseous knuckles of brilliant green? No. Lower. Back to this world. Not a smell anymore. Something to feel. Feeling again. A well of shocking nerves from her left ankle just above her missing foot. Where was her foot? She lifted her head. The brightest white. Brighter than child ghosts' bleached shorts. Her own little star gnashing bright through the darkness. This star was hers.

Sloan made his way down first, deftly jumping the gap in the rungs. Topper followed now. He descended slowly, prolonging his feet planting on the metal grates of the catwalk. He didn't want to see. He was all about ladies in their underwear, but he didn't want to see how they could be damaged. When he finally reached the floor, his stomach lurched. A tiny, sharp bone jutted through the arch of her foot. It glowed, slick from blood in the moonlight. Like a star. They were hard to come by. It had been since last summer that he'd been far enough out of the city to see stars. His girlfriend at the time, she was sixteen and drove a Firebird, the younger sister of one of his brother's girls, had taken him to a golf course in Augusta. No streetlights, no orange glow in the sky, only stars and blackness as they lay on their backs against a finely mowed putting green. He never knew how littered the sky was with stars, bright pin pricks. He made it to third base that night. Warm, dark places and brilliance.

But it was obvious that this woman was in a bad way. She was mumbling now. When he got himself to look at her again, her breasts, covered in a black bra, were invisible, camouflaged in darkness. Her waist gone in black, too. But that tiny bone was so white. It's what stopped her from being swallowed.

"I said it before, man, and now it's really time," Topper said. "We gotta jet."

"We can't leave her." Sloan touched the woman's forehead, feeling her temperature with the back of his hand as his mother might do. He scooped the bangs from her eyes. "*We* did this."

"No, man. *She* did this to herself. We should've left her where we found her."

"Then I'll just call an ambulance. The cops maybe."

"Are you hell-bent on fucking yourself? Bad shit will happen to us if you call the cops."

"Help me get her out of here, or I won't have a choice."

"Then what?" Topper cinched up his shorts. He was getting cold. He wanted to put his clothes back on. It was this lady, this damn junkie, who had him standing there stripped. And now she threatened to expose them further. He'd be paraded through the neighborhood in his underwear, highlighted by flashing blue and red, face down in shadows like his dad. Or like his brother, who'd gone to jail for a white woman. His brother couldn't have hurt a woman. He loved women, just as Topper did. The wrong place with the wrong people and you got assumptions, court dates, rulings, permanent records. Nothing you did after could erase. This woman wasn't worth it. He wished Sloan wasn't so stupid. He wished Sloan wasn't so good. "I can see how this is gonna turn out, and all of it ends with fucking me over."

"It's not all about you."

"You're a straight-A student." Topper made a circle with his thumb and index finger and puckered into it. "A little ass kiss. Clean record. They'll pin this shit on me. So, yeah, it's *all* about me." It was half-true. Half to save his ass, but the other half was for Sloan, his stupid friend and his perfect grades.

"We were trying to help."

"Yeah, and I bet that's exactly how they'll see it," Topper said. "You're so blind. Two black kids strip a white woman and bust her up. Junkie or not, she's white. White is right, man."

"Will you stop with that shit?"

"Don't leave me," the woman said.

The boys' eyes darted to her body, a dripping puddle on the catwalk, tapping echoes onto the hollow boilers below. Her eyes and mouth were still closed. It seemed impossible for her to speak, like a baby sister's first words.

"What do you want us to do, lady?" Sloan asked.

"Don't make me dust. I want more stars." She trailed off.

"See, man. She's crazy," Topper said.

"Let's get her out of here."

The boys carried her by thighs and arms over and down the labyrinthine catwalks, toward the window on the second floor. They retied the clothes rope around her. Topper climbed out first to help from the ground. It was cold and late. He stood in front of his sleeping neighborhood, wearing nothing but shorts. He thought about bolting, felt his legs throb full of adrenaline. It would be so easy to leave it all in Sloan's hands. He might not get in much real trouble. He couldn't risk screwing up Sloan's life, though, abandoning the pride of their neighborhood—exemplary student, mower of lawns, half-white—which had so little to be proud about. He hated his friend for making him care too much.

Millie Bliss leaned her elbows on her knees. She'd been waiting an endless hour for boys to emerge men.

One of the boys darted out a window of the powerhouse, slicing through the night in white shorts. Another body, gleaming with yellow streetlights, spilled through the same window. It didn't move with the nimbleness of the boys. It floated like an angel.

Where there was whiteness on the boys, blackness. Blackness across the waist and chest, refusing the yellow glow. This was no angel. Something sick and evil. The humid attic air caught heavy in her chest.

She couldn't stand the weakness of her night vision, the weakness of distance that the cold lenses of her dead husband's binoculars could not cure. The toes of her boots tapped against each other. She pulled at the wrinkles in her neck. Angels with black waists and one missing boy promised a disaster. She knew it.

In her husband's closet, she found a black overcoat. She slipped a metal flashlight into one of the long pockets. Down the steps, she grabbed from the wall the small crucifix with the ivory Jesus; she'd need faith to face black angels. Near her front door, she grabbed her house keys, some matches, a photo of her husband in uniform holding an ice-cream cone—a man and a boy all in one. She put everything she could find into those pockets. Everything she might need to save the boys and the neighborhood: a handful of red-and-white mints, a hairbrush, a screwdriver, a hand towel, two spoons, her orange bottle of codeine. She swept through the door and across Belford Street. Past the houses and through the chain-link fence surrounding the powerhouse lot.

Millie Bliss flattened against a wall of the powerhouse. She peered around the side. The hunched angel, at this point, was landing in the fingertips of one of the boys. She was no angel. A young woman in her underwear, the boy in his shorts. The flying, merely a dangle of clumped, knotted fabrics. It was all parlor tricks. Deception led to sin. Sin, to disaster. All the important things in her pockets felt heavy. This would be a matter of subtraction, not addition. She needed to remove the sin, save the boys.

"Okay, I got her." Topper's whispers hissed alongside a lonely car rushing by on the street. "Get down here and take your woman."

Sloan tossed the rope of clothes and then jumped down. He felt so close to finishing now. He'd done the search, the rescue, now what? He took the lady from his friend's arms.

Topper picked up the rope and worked at the knots. To get his jeans free, he had to untangle Sloan's T-shirt and the woman's pants. To get his shirt, he had to loosen the knuckles that bound it to Sloan's cargos. Everything was so fucking connected. A mess of knots. Why didn't Sloan care about the tangles? The neighborhood could wake at any moment. All he wanted was to get his clothes free and get this thing over with. He felt small in his shorts and cold. The early a.m. chill of the late summer tightened his balls into an infant's fist. He only had one leg of his pants free. The knot connecting to Sloan's shirt refused to give.

"Boys your age shouldn't be out so late," Millie Bliss said, walking toward Sloan.

Topper yanked at the one pant leg he had free. He thrust his other foot into the hole still knotted tight, but as hard as he pushed, he couldn't pull the pants to his waist. He stumbled to a standing position, gripping his jeans with tensed fingers. The clothes rope tailed at his feet, a shadow he couldn't escape. But the intruder in their night paid little attention to Topper. She spoke to his friend.

"Sloan, how are your parents?"

"Fine, Mrs. Bliss."

"You better get home to them, or they won't be so fine."

"Mrs. Bliss, it's not what it looks like." Topper stepped between the two of them, still struggling to keep his knotted pants up. "Sloan, and me too, we were trying to help. You don't need to tell our parents, get anyone else involved."

She nodded and smiled, as if he were someone she'd known all her life. The recognition made him shudder.

"Who else should be involved?" she asked. "I'll bring my car around and take care of this mess."

"Thanks, Mrs. Bliss." Topper swung the tail of clothes rope over his shoulder.

"I'll be back in a minute." She eyed both of them. "No more trouble until then, boys."

Sloan stood straight, holding the woman. He could hold her all night if he had to. He had the strength to figure out what to do next, without Mrs. Bliss's help. The woman was out again. Jupiter or Pluto, as Topper said. Sloan could see her better now under the hazy glow of streetlight that never let their street be truly dark. Her lips were pale, cracked, and peeling. Roots of blonde crowned the peak of her head, spilling into a brunette dye. Her lungs rattled softly through her back, against the palm of his right hand. Warmth slipped into his left. Like the piss before, but blood this time, from her skinned knee. Lower, there was the foot he'd ruined. Would the blood be scalding at the bone that popped from her foot? A core of brilliant magma. He felt the weight lightening. Finishing becoming a mystery. Out of his hands. Soon into Mrs. Bliss's wrinkled fingers, which could not be as strong as his.

The boys watched Millie Bliss's red Lincoln roll up and stop at the perimeter of the chain-link fence. Topper slapped his friend's shoulder. "Come on, man. Let's get this shit over with."

Topper hustled ahead to the car. Sloan followed, taking slow steps. Topper couldn't handle the weight Sloan held in his arms, even though he was taller. Topper was weak, a quitter. Here they had a chance to do something good, something that mattered.

At the car, Topper opened the passenger-side door, waving Sloan forward.

"Right there is fine, boys," Millie said, pointing to the seat. Sloan hesitated, but she kept her finger pointed, eying him with a look she might give a child, waiting for him to surrender a slingshot. She made no reference to the woman. Her weight burned in his arms. He lowered her.

Through squinted eyelashes, Alex looked up at him again. Magnificent white eyes against a black sky. She was being released. Gods' regrets became a soft gravity onto upholstery. Her neck rolled. Windshield. Digital clock. Steering wheel. Chariot. Canoe down River Styx so much like a car. An old woman full of cold. Her wrinkles made ghosts and gods seem like boys. And she had nothing to give for fare to the old woman. Maybe it had already been paid. Maybe she was already too far in debt from stealing for anyone to care. She didn't want to leave. But this was not her place. Goodbye to sky and almost stars, to crumbling history.

"Good boy." Mrs. Bliss turned the key, rumbling the Lincoln to life.

"Her clothes are still tied up over here." Sloan pointed to the tail of clothes over Topper's shoulder.

"I'll take care of her now. She won't need those tatters."

"So we're good then?" Topper asked.

"That's up to you two," she said. "You young boys, running around in your underwear, playing games. You'll catch a cold. Get dressed and go home."

Goosebumps sprouted over Sloan's arms. He felt chilled for the first time that night. The light hairs on his arms stood up, stained in the lady's blood and piss.

"Sloan, be sure to get to my lawn this week. It's embarrassing how long it is. God only knows what the neighbors think. I expect you to stay on top of things like that."

And that was his place. Gifted gardener, grass and grass alone. He watched Mrs. Bliss and the woman creep down the street.

"I'm done with knots." Topper slung what was left of the clothes rope around Sloan's neck. His shirt and pants were finally untangled and free. The last knots bound Sloan's clothing to the woman's. "I'm done with this shit, too. Junkies and the mill. I'm going home."

"What do you think Mrs. Bliss will do?" Sloan sank to a squat and yanked at his clothes, fumbling slowly with his cold, filthy fingers. "Take her to the hospital?"

"Fuck if I know. Hell if I care. We should just be glad she came along. I mean, what would we have done with her? You didn't know."

"We'd have figured something out."

The Lincoln turned the corner of the lot, toting the woman he was supposed to save.

"Well, there you go, man. She's going to a better place."

"Why you gotta say it like that?"

"Junkie heaven in a Lincoln. Down to the methadone clinic in style. What lucky trash."

Topper didn't get it, couldn't understand how close they'd been to doing something important, to finishing something. The lady was nothing to him but stupid jokes he'd learned from his loser brother. Sloan's hands tightened into stones. He swung his fist into the side of Topper's face. He'd been waiting all night for this to come to a conclusion, and here it was. This was how it would end, the descent from a mountain. His friend with no feelings, flat on his ass.

On the ground, Topper held his face, sucked cool air through his teeth. He watched Sloan pull his shirt over his head, step into his pants. And in that second, blood filling Topper's mouth, Sloan looked strong like his brother. But would Sloan ever understand the important thing—that no one cared? This neighborhood, this city, Mrs. Bliss, no one gave a fuck about one good deed that wouldn't change a thing. Better to give up and duck out. Mrs. Bliss knew. She'd lived here too long not to know. If she saved this woman, finished what Sloan started and took her to the hospital, there would have to be explanations. She could get in trouble. They could get in trouble. Mrs. Bliss wasn't that stupid. She'd take the woman far enough, out of their neighborhood, and dump her. Away from them, where her body didn't have the strength to tear anyone in this neighborhood apart. Maybe that was close enough to one good deed.

BUILDING WALLS

FORGET EIGHT HOURS, LUNCH BREAKS, SMOKE BREAKS, BATH-
room breaks. This is a twelve-hour mother. Boss Sleeth gives our
crew one day to finish this house. He's trying out the boys from
Mexico, and if we can't finish fast as them, some of us might not
survive. We like their work, those boys from Mexico, who we know
are actually from Colombia, farther south than Boss Sleeth imagines. They swing mud good as we've seen, good as we do. We like
their brown skin against so much gray Sheetrock. Makes us think
of sun. We won't see sun today, except for a mushy glow through
the plastic-masked windows. Same windows, same bulkheads and
bullnose corners, same walls we've finished so many times that
our hands don't need our eyes. But today we must be faster. Faster
than men, than ourselves, than boys from Mexico. Today is ours
to get through. Our walls to build. We push into this house in the
subdivision before dawn, before dew, before the moon drops like
a cannonball through a boat hull. Hot sizzle into ocean like blue
sky. Steam and bubbles.

Bubbles. We forget about those. We don't see soap. Even when
our hands ache for clean. Like when Ivan pitched a pile of dead
possum babies from between the framing joists. Hairless things as
pink as fiberglass insulation. Pink on top, turning brown against

the studs. Dead brown. Brown like the rust chewing up Bubba's stilts. Started at the bottom of his stilt struts, a spot or two, but rust climbs all the way up to the platforms now, where he stands in dirty, ratty Reebok sneakers with a hole fraying the right big toe. We worry about that hole. Worry maybe rust'll get tired of chomping on cold aluminum, and once it finds Bubba's soft right toe with the split nail from when he dropped a five bucket of mud on it, the rust might crawl all the way up his leg. Maybe if he took off those stilts now and then. But he doesn't. We're not sure he can walk without them. Bubba's always first on-site. Stilted up before we arrive. Won't touch ground for twelve hours. Maybe thirteen today. Got to finish with the mudding to give the walls time to dry. Time like we never get. Always more walls for us, so long as we beat the boys from Mexico. These here walls need to be finished and dry. Tomorrow, Stags does his sanding thing.

Ever seen Stags do his sanding thing? It's beautiful, like Christmas. Limestone snow falling all around. Chokes us up. But not because we're thinking of that Christmas we got what we always wanted, that green thing that floated in the tub and was shaped like a boat but had knobby wheels too so you could push it through the dirt. That was before this thirteen-hour mother and all the mothers before it. That was a long time ago, when we scrubbed our soft hands in washtubs while Momma lifted us on her knee so we could reach and see all the tiny rainbows in the bubbles. Different kind of snow. Stags's snow creeps into our lungs so sly we don't even know, until we're hacking up snakes of white.

Snow was pretty once. We hold on to that. We hope we don't forget and hope Stags's snow doesn't work into our brains and smooth out those wrinkles.

Stags will never be replaced. Too cheap for Boss Sleeth. Stags picks up his kids from school and brings them to wintertime. Stags's crew: eight-year-old What's-His-Face and nine-year-old Pigtails. They know how to work the sanding pole. They know how to make snow. They know how to snap on a paper mask, and we hope they don't forget to snug the straps both above their ears and around their necks. Please don't forget to bend the little metal piece over your nose. That kind of snow's no good. Keep your masks tight.

Stags and his wintertime crew sand tomorrow. So today we drag our trowels careful as surgeons, because that means fewer ridges, less snowmaking for those kids. We take our time. We do it right, even if that means too slow for Sleeth.

No sun for us. Shaping into a fourteen-hour mother.

John is just John. Never called him no different, maybe because of the pink line sledding down his cheekbone under his right eye. A wave of missing skin. A flesh trough. A rut. John is just John, and you better not call him anything else. John keeps a baggy of little snowballs like Stags makes except it's different stuff, chokes you up in another different way. If we don't call John anything but John, he might share some, in the basement, among walls of stone, which don't need Sheetrock and mud and Stags's sanding. Someone else made these walls. We don't think about how they did it, whether they survived. We just know we have walls around us to block out the wind so John can take the first hit out of a pipe he made by crinkling tinfoil around his pinkie finger. John passes it to us, and if we're one of the ones who do that sort of thing and if we're lucky and John is generous enough to load up his finger pipe with enough snowball stuff, then we'll clutch it in our lungs as long as we can, until we grow strong enough to fight the thirteen motherfucking hours waiting for us upstairs.

What happened to fourteen?

Well, we filled a few screw holes, and Bubba's on his stilts, knocking out the ceiling. That's one less hour. It has to be.

John is not one of us. He's one of Ivan's Sheetrock-hanging boys. They're almost done on the second floor, almost done hanging and hammering more walls for us to finish. Thunder overhead. Ivan won't slow down our mudding and taping. Ivan has a crew of seven, more of them than us. We'll miss him and his boys when they leave, when they go to the next house, hang Sheetrock for the boys from Mexico so they can sling mud faster than us. This is not Ivan's betrayal. Not when there are always more walls. We understand Ivan. We love Ivan. He sings to us, *Nobody does it better*. He tells us, if we worked for him, he'd under-the-table us fat bonuses and deport us to vacationland. Ivan grins like he's breaking rocks with his molars.

Ivan has a bald spot flashing through his thick black hair. Bald in just one place, on the top of his head. Bubba sees it best from his stilts. A perfect circle the size of a fist. Not from getting old, Ivan says. And Papa in Russia has a full mop of gray hair. Ivan's bald from lugging Sheetrock with his skull. His head can carry three stacked quarter-inch sheets, only two half-inch sheets. Heavy mothers. Hair can't grow under that pressure. But that's how diamonds do it. Lots of pressure. Time and more time. Some of us still believe it could be elephants stomping coal off in Africa. That's fairytale. And so is Africa and Russia and maybe Mexico and definitely diamonds.

Except for Gordy. Gordy has a ring on layaway at JCPenney. Thirteen more hours is fine for him. Just fine. That's another layaway payment. Big sparkling hunk of stone. Platinum band. Going to give it to his gal. Gordy must survive Sleeth's test. We have to finish faster than the boys from Mexico for him. Only six more payments. We don't want diamonds to turn fairytale for Gordy. Fairytales make our teeth itch, forearms tense, make us wish we hadn't wasted time with John, even though we needed that to make us faster, those of us who need that sort of thing anyway.

Gordy's gal brings him lunch or dinner or breakfast. We don't know which until he snaps open the plastic container. We smell eggs. Eggs and corned-beef hash. Eggs with Tabasco sauce like drops of blood and hash with coagulated ketchup. It's breakfast, then. Smells so good, but the smell creeps into our spines, into our insteps, into our incisors, and it hurts because that means we've only hit morning, only a few hours in and still don't even have all the screw holes filled. Back to where we started, twelve hours at least.

John stops throwing Sheetrock scraps out the window upstairs, carries them down and out the front door instead, eying Gordy's gal the whole time. Breathing her in, eggs and hash and Tabasco and—there it is, flowers, perfume smelling like lilacs. We forgot about flowers.

Bubba likes the smell, too, but that's all he gets. Just a whiff. Strapped into rusty stilts, up high, eyes blind to Gordy's gal, eyes full of wall, full of ceiling, gray Sheetrock and white mud and the occasional flash of silver trowel, speck or two of brown where the rust has sneaked up his blade. He doesn't look at Gordy's gal, only walls. Same should go for all of us. And that's why Gordy doesn't steal his gal out to her car, why he feels safe powwowing with her on the plywood subfloors. We don't gawk, because we have to keep working or we'll never finish in time to save Gordy and his gal and their diamonds.

That doesn't mean we don't cheat looks. We scoop our trowels into our pans a little more often, linger a little longer in the mud. Only time we get to look away from the wall. Time we get to look at Gordy's gal's brown hair frizzing out its ponytail, fingernails painted orange and chipped, the zipper of her sweatshirt sprouting a flash of yellow tank top over a trail of shadow where one breast meets another.

Is Gordy's gal beautiful? It's eleven more hours, and we will not see another woman. She is the most beautiful thing we've ever seen, and we all want to give her diamonds on layaway at JCPenney. We want Gordy's gal forever and always, until this fourteen-hour mother is over.

Gordy's Gal leaves and Ivan leaves, John and his snowballs and eggs and hash and Tabasco with them. Boss Sleeth returns. Big and round and too much face to grow a mustache. Boss tries. A black hair here and there, like the mustaches we grew when we were fourteen. Bubba grew a beard at fourteen. Bubba was taller than stilts at fourteen. Bubba's blond beard makes Boss Sleeth impatient, waiting for his upper lip to grow in, waiting for us to finish the walls.

He says, Daddy Sleeth is here now, boys. He says, Daddy Sleeth will help you boys finish what you need discipline and proper management to complete in a timely manner. Always milking me, you boys, not like my Mexican boys. But I don't have shit for you boys to milk today. See, see. He pulls his pockets inside out and leaves them hanging.

We do not take our eyes away from the walls. We don't want to see Boss Sleeth's empty pockets or his work. He picks up the spare trowel, heaps mud into a pan, jams mud into the cracks in the front door, seals it tight.

No one leaves until we finish, he says. This door is a wall now, see, he says. These windows are not windows but just gaps in a world you can't leave until you finish, which won't be until tomorrow at your rate. I want you boys to win, you see. Brown friends and white brothers. I love you all, but you are my boys, you see. I do this to get the best out of you.

He slaps mud over screw holes we've already filled, over seams we've already smoothed. New ridges. Big humps. Stags's kids will have extra sanding, will learn about mothers of days tomorrow after they learn in school about how they can't leave until the clock hands swing a certain way. When they grow up, Boss Sleeths will tally clock ticks, will squint at time cards, will show them the insides of pockets as white as milk. They have grown up already, though. They have snow-scarred lungs. A blister grew and popped and hardened on Pigtail's palm under her ring finger.

Only Bubba's work is safe from Boss Sleeth. Boss doesn't climb ladders, wear stilts. Too big. Massive. Stomping the subfloor like Ivan-thunder around us, behind us, where we don't dare to look.

Trowels and pans too slow for Boss Sleeth, he takes up the banjo—expensive equipment Boss bought to sail through his mothers of days. Small mothers for him. Daughters who play house with dolls and pink tea sets for him. The banjo is a box of shiny metal, mud and tape in one swing. No pick or twang from this banjo. No music. Not to Boss Sleeth anyway. We listen to the mud. We hear it hum: Too wet, too dry, bubbling from the inside. Mud sings: Too heavy, too light, tape's going to slide. A language in clicks and squishes, something like crickets.

Boss Sleeth is too loud to listen. He clanks his banjo, smashes into corners, zips through horizontal seams. We dodge Boss Sleeth when he comes our way. Pins to his bowling ball. Sleeth's banjoing slops our seams. He writes the checks. He hires boys from Mexico, not caring they're from Colombia. What can we do? Some of us sneak upstairs to work on Ivan's newly hung rooms. Away from Boss Sleeth. Some of us need that. Some of us want to see Boss work, remind ourselves who's milking who.

Mud's too thin, too much water in the mix, drips out the banjo box. We hear trickle and plop. We don't say anything. He sees his pants streaked wet and gray. His face reddens. He says, Fuck, hurls the banjo. Banjo breaks into shiny fragments littering the subfloor like veins of silver. If we were miners, shiny would matter. We're not miners. We watch the mud spilled and lumped, hope not too much was lost. Picking up another five bucket would add an hour. We've already worked six, or seven, or four. Doesn't matter. Only the mud on the walls matters. Our walls and the boys from Mexico's walls. We hope Boss helps them too.

Boss Sleeth says, There's no managing you boys. He breaks through his mudded front door. When he slams it behind him, dried mud shards fall like broken teeth. We exhale. We smile. No one recovers the broken banjo. Let silver shine until the sun is gone. We dream of seeing that sun refracted in the pieces of Boss's tantrum.

Silver shine dims and dies.

Sal rumbles up the hopper, untangles the hose. Time for more snow that isn't snow. Finished with the main floor finishing. Sal will spray texture from the hopper, and Bubba will knock it down. More stilt work, always on the stilts.

Sal crosses his arms over the bucket of water. Water to thin the mud for texture. Clean, clear water for the hopper. For us, no water. Sal's 102-ounce soda squats in the corner, impossibly still has ice. We hear it jingle in Sal's grip. Sal shares with no one.

Sal went to the dentist yesterday. First time in seven years. Black gaps between each tooth. Those dentists cleaned away most of his white. We want to fill his mouth with mud, because we are scared of teeth cleaned so thin. Scared of soda. Thirsty for the water Sal cracks open for the hopper.

The hopper won't share its mud-mixing water either. But when the bucket is empty, we will have a bathroom. No sooner. We squeeze our thighs. We tell ourselves, Three more walls and then we shit. We lie to our bodies. Always more walls.

We wonder if the boys from Mexico brought water. Seven-gallon coolers sweating pearls, stacks of little paper cups that must be refilled again and again. We peer through the dimming masked windows and hope they have water, hope they refill frequently, piss constantly. Healthy kidneys and slower finishing.

Sal squirms into a tissue-paper jumpsuit. He clicks on the flood lamps, makes the gloaming outside turn black. Dreams of sun disappear. He smiles with thin teeth as tight as Ivan's rock crushers. Time for texture means this mother is almost done. It means we must soon leave these walls for walls at home. Apartments and duplexes and Gordy's two-story rental. Can't touch the walls at home. Lease states this clearly. We've checked. Page 5, right after the part about running a meth lab. These walls, we can touch. These ones may save us from stealing the painters' five-gallon buckets of paint thinner so we can start meth labs.

Sal sprays white hell from the hopper, pretends he's firing an automatic from the hip, then pretends the hose is his dick. Bubba doesn't laugh. He sits on the scaffold while Gordy kneels below him to fiddle with the stilt's rusty notches. We remember how hard it was to tie our shoes in first grade, how we almost flunked because of the tie-your-shoe test. The terror of flunking, of next year being taller than everyone else. Billy Cobin charged us a quarter to retie our shoes if they came undone during kickball. Gordy doesn't charge a thing. He notches down Bubba's stilts. Shorter so Bubba can work the giant plexi knock-down knife. Bigger knife means shorter Bubba. Shorter Bubba means he's closer to standing on the subfloor with his own dirty sneakers, caked in drying mud, gazing up at all the walls he's finished.

Bubba grips the rusty metal frame of the scaffold while Gordy slides up his struts below. Bubba's palm turns brown, but he doesn't notice. When he rubs his brow, a swatch of rust smears his forehead. No water to clean the rust away. The rust will stay until we're done.

How long until we're done?

Gordy wants to ask, but he knows better.

Done when we walk out the front door, when we win against the boys from Mexico. But winning is walking through another door. Through our own doors to more walls. Walls we didn't build together. Walls that surround us, each one.

WORKMEN'S COMPENSATION

INDICATIONS: FOR THE TEMPORARY RELIEF OF TEN-HOUR days, including demoing triple-layer shingles, spreading felt and nailing shingles, or spreading tar or rolling rubber. Will ease shame of your denied raise, neglect of your grids' perfect symmetry. Paychecks will miraculously appear without scabbed kneecaps and a kinked spine, sunburned scalp and aching ankles. During daylight, you can wear sweatpants or underwear or nothing at all, instead of jeans hardened in tar. You will decrease proximity to the sun, and daylight will become full of opportunity. More time, time, time.

DIRECTIONS: A hammer will do. A hammer balanced on top of your ladder ready to fall when you hoist it against your chest. Or stand atop the second-to-last step, or allow the feet to slide, or use that hammer to bash the safety stop. These are just a few ladder options. Here's another: Prolong stares at your coworker Camille while she straddles the peak, stretching to nail cap, revealing the olive skin on her lower back. Daydream about fucking against hot shingles, bending her over the fresh porcelain in the half bath, lifting her body against the cinderblocks of the basement. Relax, remember to breathe, and let the ladder do the rest.

ACTIVE INGREDIENTS: Gravity, cudgel, fear of OSHA, disorientation, daydreams and fantasies, aluminum, mineral spirits, nailer, worn sneaker tread, desire.

SIDE EFFECTS: Days may appear longer at home. Too long. Vitamin D intake drops when your blinds are always closed. Paranoia induced by the man wearing the hard hat who drives slowly past your window, who snaps pictures when you peep through the slats. You cannot understand why he wears a hard hat while driving. Try blinking to make sure your vision is clear. He may be out to catch you, he may be out to kill you, he may become something like a coworker if you bring him coffee. But remember to suck air through your teeth, clutch your side. Or just stay inside and think of Camille. Think of her knocking on your apartment door, begging you to come back because no one else asks about her big plans for the weekend, about her six-year-old son's T-ball game. No one else can make her happy. But only consider; don't envision. Avoid hallucination. Avoid hallucinating hard hats.

DIRECTIONS: Stepping on a nail is not enough. Prolonged disablement is your goal. But not permanence. The balance between lasting and forever is delicate but essential. The eave borders are easy to forget when working backward, a quick slip over fascia and soffit. Your fall must appear accidental, but remember to plan. Combine falls with pine trees or shrubs, compost piles or full dumpsters. Land on legs and not your neck. Practice on your mother's gabled ranch that your father built but didn't have time to reshingle before dying. When the time comes, a one-story roof will not be enough, and three stories are too much. Remember to cry for Camille when you land. Remember to groan. Use your diaphragm. Choke and gurgle through your punctured lung.

CONSULT DOCTOR: If erections last longer than four hours. If Camille never appears at your threshold but never leaves your mind. Seek holistic treatment: lubricant, callused grip, Camille's kerchief, magazines, movies. You have time now. Go to the bar and drink and drink. Go to the bar and buy drink after drink for the woman who will lean on your shoulder, squeeze your bicep, sneak you into the women's bathroom. If ejaculation does not erase desire, do not return to work. Several days and shifts and weeks and months may pass before you lose feeling. You have plenty of time for Camille to fade. Consider compounding your claim into emotional distress.

SIDE EFFECTS: The man in the hard hat will drive by and snap pictures at dawn, your old punch-in time. He creeps up to your front door. You watch him through the peephole, and all you see is hard hat. It is white, a sticker of the American flag pasted on the stubby bill, part of it scratched away to fuzzy gum. When you open the door carrying Pop-Tarts, he has disappeared. Only the white hard hat sits on your front step, and you have no use for that. He will not be your friend. You realize you're not as close to your coworkers as you thought. They do not call, do not visit. You will long for their voices bounding over the ridge, will long for the swoon of a fresh bucket of tar, for the flesh of plywood turned black and sparkling, for the simple clarity of chalk-line grids. Resist. Resist these small satisfactions from the time when you worked for the hour. Enjoy your clean fingernails, your peeling skin, the paleness underneath. Seek distraction. Get a hobby. Boats in a bottle, astrophysics, sea monkeys, pottery, but no roofing.

STORAGE: Keep in a cool, dry place. Avoid direct sunlight or even the indirect sunlight squeezing through the cracks of your blinds; you've earned shadows. Stay away from windows and hard hats. Remain indoors. Sign up for direct deposit, an option before impossible when you cashed the wrinkled checks your boss scratched out in his third-grade cursive, numbers the bank teller squinted at, asked her manager to confirm, too much cash to place in your grease-stained palms. Avoid interaction, questions, chitchat, and philosophy. You and Camille talked about starting your own roofing outfit and supernovas and circumcisions and underwater caves and skipping out of work just as you used to skip out of high school. You and her, crawling across the felt, swinging your legs over the rake and onto the ladder, then off to the beach to fry. Forget the conversations that made you sweat. Replace with the rattle of your air conditioner.

INDICATIONS: Your pottery is lopsided, but don't call it failure. You'll learn to enjoy the higher arts. Reassess the caving lid on the vase you name Mother, the lopsided plate you title Father before kneading it back into a ball, the sunbaked ashtray shaped like a diamond you consider leaving at Camille's front door. You know she smokes, but you don't know where she lives. Now you have time to gain real knowledge. Improve your mind. Read the encyclopedias your father bought when you were five that still consider Pluto valid, that end the presidents at Ford. You've lugged them to every new home, and now there is time. Don't visit your mother or succumb to the guilt of her leaking roof. Guard your precious hours and blame your spine, your fractured shin, your sprained wrist, your emotional distress. She may be the root. Just look at that caving vase. Crush that ashtray. Don't think about Camille. Stop trying to face the man in the hard hat.

DIRECTIONS: A hand slipped in hot tar is a start, but the whole cooking bucket dumped across your legs is more effective. Avoid your lap, which may lead to erectile dysfunction. Pass, for once, on drinking the cans of Coors that Camille doles out after lunch. Your claim could be threatened by inebriation. Listen to the empties plink over the eave and fight your dry tongue. Drink water. Chug your gallon warm as piss from sitting in the sun. Your gallon that once held milk, then water, the jug that looks identical to the one where your boss stores mineral spirits. Drink mineral spirits. Your nights at the pub, shots of Jameson lined up across the oak bar, they were all practice for this. Open your throat, swallow, and then hack. Blame improper storage. Unlabeled spirits that burned the tar off your hands and now burn your esophagus. You won't need your voice when you have time.

SIDE EFFECTS: Rectal bleeding, uncontrolled vomiting, a liquid diet. What goes in must come out. Difficulty swallowing, like shingles in your throat. Swollen tongue, oral blisters, inarticulation or complete inability to speak. But silence is not all bad.

EXCUSE: It's not that you won't answer your mother's calls about the mold, the puddles in her carpet; you can't.

EXCUSE: If you found Camille's home, showed up at her door, it's not that you wouldn't know what to say; your tongue can't form the words.

EXCLUSION: When the man in the hard hat whispers through your vents at night, quizzes you with his questionnaires, you don't have to lie. You shake your head, shiver and blink, curl your fingers and toes, but he can't read what you mime. He can't see through the blinds and the garbage bags you duct-taped over the windows. He relies on his ears sprouting from under his hard hat, and you can't explain.

CONSULT: Dead father, sodden mother, pretend lover. They will not hear you. There is only you and the man in the hard hat, who has taken to sleeping in his van in your parking lot. His hard hat has changed to blue, bobs over his brow as he breathes deep. You strain a whisper through your gravelly throat, through the slice of his cracked window, coax him, the power of somnambulistic suggestion. You are ready to return to work, to Camille, to ladder rungs and rooftops. You plead. But have you had enough time? He checks boxes in his sleep, his pen waving over his clipboard to the rhythm of his gentle snoring. Three more months of compensation. You beg for a stack of shingles balanced over your shoulder, but you will remain weightless. Why can't you just enjoy extra time?

SIDE EFFECTS: You were advised to ignore your mother's mossy shingles, but here you are, lugging your cast over the peak. The trouble is the ladder, how long it takes you to carry up shingles, to carry your broken body. The trouble is the silence of working alone, no distraction, time flattening out and spreading like rolls of black felt. The trouble is no Camille. You take three times as long to secure the drip edge, to sculpt the valley, to bend the flashing. And you can't discover the leak, the weakness left by your father. You slog on, cooking your new pale skin. Your mother pushes sunscreen; you've never needed it before. How many red blisters must sprout before the man in the hard hat drives by and sees you are able? He abandoned his stakeout at your apartment complex, and he doesn't show up here, at the home your father built, the shed with the single forty-five degree slope where he aimed the BB gun at your thigh to show you how the neighbor's dog felt. Shot in the leg, and you still had to mow the lawn. No escape from work. Now no man in the hard hat to see your work, to send you back.

DIRECTIONS: The nail gun provides accuracy. Stigmatic left hand or foot looks bad but heals quickly, and there's always the right. Disengage safety catch so nails can fire without surface pressure. Camille will do one of her pretend holdups: "Gimme all your flashing, or else." You raise your hands to the sun and smile. She squints, shakes away strands of loose bangs, quick draws the nailer, and aims for your chest. Without the catch, the nail releases. You watch its painfully slow trajectory. Enough time for Camille's eyes to pop, lips to spread. Three inches of galvanized steel buries into your chest. Three inches are plenty to pinprick an organ. Ignore the Spanish that spills from Camille like a sparrow shrieking in a cat's jaw. Ignore the creases in her forehead, her quivering hands, the dropped nailer that somersaults over the eave, the sound of plastic shattering on concrete. Camille has freed you. Camille's fingers feel you, squeeze your breast, press a blue kerchief into your wound.

INACTIVE INGREDIENTS: Safety catch, calluses, trust in the tools you know, guilt, prayer, emergency room, the doctor's pliers so much shinier than any tool you've ever held, your sunburned body.

STORAGE: Rest in soft places. Seek comfort. Couch to recliner to bed replaces truck bed to five-gallon bucket to roof cap. At the end of your last fourteen-hour shift, you and Camille collapsed on the freshly shingled roof, watched, on your backs, dusk paint the clouds pink. No pitch could tip you. After so many hours on tilted ground—thirty degrees, forty-five, sixty—gravity changes; bodies acclimate to angle. Impossible to fall. Now you require zero degrees. Flat and soft and alone, and yet you worry this flat world will swallow you.

SYMPTOMS: Have you forgotten all that time can do for you? You drag the utility blade across your cast, sprinkling the carpet with white flakes all evening. At twelve dollars per hour, you would have made forty-eight dollars, but why are you calculating? You no longer work for hours, time cards, crinkled personal checks, don't need to. Your leg underneath the cast is pale, shrunken, streaked in blood where you pushed the knife too deep. You tear the bandages from your chest, scrape the blackened scab, long for the shiny nail head Camille planted there. You drink a beer because you are thirsty and you're sick of water and milk. Your throat burns. You call your own answering machine and practice listening—to your own voice, to any voice, saying, I feel better. I'm ready. I'm sorry. You play the message over and over and wonder if those tin-can words are really yours.

INTERACTIONS: The man in the hard hat no longer stalks you, but you've tracked him down. Your gift of time was spent this way, circling, hunting Camille. And when you couldn't find her, you found him, the man in the hard hat's van parked on a hill. He is not inside, but two hard hats lie stacked on the passenger's seat: a white one, his blue sleeping hat. You lean on his bumper and stretch your arms, pink and raw from reshingling your mother's roof. Your skin betrays you, leaks heat, and fall is here, then winter and snow and no more roofs. The hill overlooks a new subdivision on one side. On the other side, the flat, black-rubber roof of apartment complexes.

Homes and houses. Leases and mortgages. All the roofs you can see are fresh, perfect. But a roof must be rotting somewhere.

The man in the hard hat appears through the pine trees. Binoculars and a camera tangle on straps around his neck. His hard hat is bright red. He doesn't see you until he is yards away. He raises his binoculars, gazes off at a framing crew in the subdivision over your shoulder, ants to you, busy and industrious and swinging hammers, climbing ladders, shooting nailers. You pick up a pebble from the road, throw it at the man's red hard hat. It plinks, and he keeps peering through the binoculars. You throw more pebbles. Nothing will stop his search, his work. You try to yell at him and choke. You try to charge him and stumble. Your chest stings at each palpitation.

The man in the hard hat aims his binoculars directly at you, and now is the time to show him your hammer, how you can still swing it, lift shingle stacks, climb any ladder. But you are too close. You are a blur crouching on the ground, coughing up blood.

OVERDOSE: Watch for the symptoms. Listless shifting from couch to bed. You carry your hatchet hammer, pound nails into the apartment walls, yank them out. Experience agnosia. More and more black holes pierce the white walls, but there is always more white. Snow outside, snow mounded on your mother's roof, probably mounded on Camille's roof, wherever she lives. You touch yourself but can't remember her skin over the shingles: anorgasmia. All the white and soft drowns the sound of hammer throws, of your mumbling, of your wanting to clink up the ladder and return to a work that is hibernating. The pleasure of time may lead to avolition, anhedonia, Antarctica, and another hour, and another. Turn on the TV, relax your fingers, and let your hammer go. Ignore the mute thump of steel hitting carpet.

TOUCHING IN TEXAS

JERRY'S NEW FRAMES PINCHED HIS NOSE AND DUG A RED WELT behind his left ear, and he realized, after an hour of staring in the rearview mirror, they were designed for girls. Too small for his face and flared a bit on the sides, they were definitely air force–issued girl glasses. So he hid them under a rock. In Wisconsin, where he was from, he could've chucked them into a leafy pile or a pond or stomped them into the mushy earth or buried them in a snow drift. In Texas, there were rocks. Rocks and thirsty dirt and hardly any cacti. He felt cheated on the cactus front when he arrived a year ago. He was over that. He had progressed to despising the stunted mesquite trees. Their naked arms twisted blackly. They were hunched skeletons sprouting sprigs of sickly green, like balding, broke-backed crones. Pathetic excuses for trees. He didn't need new glasses to see them any better. Certainly not cat-eyed, welt-inducing frames.

He'd driven to the outskirts of town, a sandy freeway overpass, far enough from his dorm on Goodfellow, where no one could find them. He hardly knew this town outside the base walls. San Angelo. This nothing place with its nothing trees where the air force had sent him to train as a fireman. His ASVAB scores were abysmal. So this was his fate. He spent his days spraying foam at burnt-out busses and helicopter husks. He was a glorified fire extinguisher. He was an idiot, and the base optician had further confirmed this by letting him select these terrible girl's frames.

Without his glasses, the red and yellow grit at his feet blended into fuzz. He wouldn't be able to spot any snakes or fire ants or whatever other hellish tortures lurked in Texas. Just as well. He only needed to survive the night, and then the air force would issue him new frames. They had to. Their fire extinguishers had to be able to see. So he had this one night of near blindness to suffer through. He wouldn't even be able look at porn on his laptop without jamming the screen against his nose. Reading was all that was left, and he'd already read the new issue of *Field and Stream* cover to cover twice. The glittering streams and camouflaged shoulders and brag photos of limp-necked bucks just made his heart ache. His brother had mailed him *The Idiot* by Dostoyevsky. He vaguely remembered Lawrence blabbing at Thanksgiving about how much his students had enjoyed being idiots, his corduroy-blazer cuffs flapping along with his excited hands. Turned out he'd said *reading The Idiot*, which was a giant book. Jerry knew his brother believed him to be dumber than his students, too dumb to even read a book about an idiot. Jerry would read it. Jerry would show him. He'd read it, and then he'd set it on fire and take pictures of the flaming pages and not put the fire out and send pictures of an eternal idiot fire to his brother.

On his way back to his rented Camaro, he stubbed his toe. He looked down and saw a mush of orange gray. The sun was setting. If he didn't make it back to his Camaro soon, night would blind him. It would be impossible for him to drive. Safely. But he didn't care about anyone in this town. Without his glasses, they all looked like the same blurs of camouflage and flesh. He'd just wanted one weekend of driving fast, wind whipping his bare chest, cruising past girls and revving a rented six-cylinder engine so loud they could feel it under their skirts. Now that plan was dead.

He skimmed his foot over the ground until he found the offending rock. It felt lighter than he had expected in his hand. Powdery and dead dry like everything else. He touched it to his nose. Just a fog of yellow. Not like the stones he'd find in Lake Michigan, green and red and stamped with ancient shell prints and bolts of quartz. This stone looked like nothing. Earth fuzz.

He heaved it toward where he imagined the road ran. It landed with a hollow thunk. And he supposed he was glad he didn't throw it in the road, didn't cause some car to careen into the ditch and burst into a ball of fire. He was so sick of fires.

"You should be more careful with your target practice," a woman's voice called from the rock's direction. "Almost noggined me."

"Yes, ma'am. Sorry, ma'am." Jerry's back shot straight. His hand almost cocked into a salute. But he stopped himself. He was off base, off duty. He couldn't know if this woman was an officer. He couldn't know if she was anything. He couldn't even locate her silhouette against the dimming gray-red dusk.

When his brother dropped him off here after basic, he'd told Jerry that you probably couldn't throw a rock without hitting an airman. So he better be careful not to do anything stupid even off the base. Lawrence was nineteen years older, the goddamn-know-everything professor, and he loved pretending to be Jerry's dad. Their dad was dead. But Lawrence was right. This town was crawling with flightless airmen.

"I come most nights to watch," she said. "Usually from my car, but then I saw you tonight. You look confused."

"Watch what, ma'am?" Jerry stepped toward the voice, the shadow. He was getting closer.

"You joking?" She sounded older, maybe in her early forties. The age of his brother's wife. They were both professors, and she was always asking what he was going to do next. "You seriously don't know, guy?" But maybe she had one of those sexy husky voices sometimes attached to girls who smoke too much and watch too many black-and-white movies and want guys to see their retro garter clips. "You're in for a treat."

He kept approaching her voice. He'd have to get so close to be able to know exactly how old she was, how blue her eyes were, how gentle the slope of her nose, how smooth her skin. He just needed her words to guide him.

"Are you alone?" Jerry asked.

"I come here almost every night. I usually stay in my car," she repeated.

Jerry was sure he had her now. The voice crystalized, each word crisp and smoky. A whiff of something citrus trailed to him and then disappeared. Just a trace. He'd know more soon. He just had to beat twilight and its total blindness.

"That's close enough," she said. Her arm rose toward him. She seemed to be aiming.

"I don't know what that is," Jerry said.

"You don't want to find out." She kept her arm raised.

He took another step, and her blurry arm jagged upward. Could be mace or a Taser or pistol, or a fucking banana for all he knew. Damn that goddamn optician for telling him he looked really cool in these frames. Just before, Jerry had asked him what it was like to work under a twentysomething with a sweet ass. Did he ever tap that? The optometrist was an officer and a woman. The optician was enlisted and a man. Where was the camaraderie? That shithead optician had screwed him over good.

Jerry charged toward her, reached out, but didn't make it farther than his sprinted third step before he tripped and tumbled through the bone-sharp tallgrass.

"What I can't tell is," the woman stood over him now, "whether you need help or you're a crazy idiot."

"I don't need help." Jerry lay on the dry earth. He squinted at her shoes, sneakers, black Converse Chucks with fraying laces. No socks. There wasn't enough light to see if her skin was wrinkly or had stretch marks. She could be retro or vintage.

"So you're a crazy idiot," she said. "That's not really the preferred choice here."

"I'm not an idiot."

"And choosing crazy's not really the better choice either." The sneakers shuffled backward. They blended back into blur.

Jerry's right elbow stung. He rolled over on his side and grabbed it. Then his lower back screamed out a similar sting. He yowled. And then he caught himself. Another stinging pinch popped, and he screeched.

"Crazy is getting confirmed," she said to his writhing body.

"Fucking fire ants," he said, "ma'am." He jumped to his feet. They were all over his back. Their tiny legs skittered across his skin, a sweet tickle that made their bite all the worse. This was the hell that was Texas.

"Stay calm and brush them off," she said. "Stop jerking around like a crazy asshole."

Jerry swatted, in spite of the woman's advice, in spite of Texas. He punched at his back, stomped the ground, clawed at his arms. He screamed. A hand clasped his shoulder, and he stopped flailing. No one had touched him in six months. The last person had been his brother, who tried to hug him when he dropped him off. Jerry had gone limp in his brother's arms and then disappeared into his dorm while his brother was still dabbing his eyes with some fancy silky kerchief.

The woman lifted his T-shirt over his head. She swiped the shirt over his back, and the stings crumbled away. Then she wiped his stomach and chest. She kept her head lowered. He couldn't see her face, only the top of her head, short hair, a side part. She moved closer, and he thought he could see lighter roots against her scalp. Natural gray or just dying for fun. He wanted to lift her face so he could see her skin, her expression, read what she really thought of him. He reached down quickly. His fingers butted into her breasts. She kneed him in his crotch, and Jerry keeled over.

"It's mace, so you know." She was away from him again, a blur again, and aiming again. "Fire ants are gonna feel like love nibbles. This is gonna burn like a motherfucker."

"Please, don't," Jerry said. He realized he was crying. Just a little. Just like his brother had faked to make him feel like shit. It was easy. It was just enough to put out this lady's fire.

"You don't go grabbing a nice lady's tits and get no payback for it."

"Sorry about that. I really am. I can't see anything is all."

"You're not blind, and even if you were, that don't give you a free tit-grabbing pass."

Behind him, where the freeway bridged over the bald earth, a wind picked up. It sounded like wind, a high-pitched whine, and he waited for the breeze against his bite-sore back. It didn't come. The wind was never a relief here. Always more hot.

The woman didn't mace him. Her arms lowered. The wind grew louder, higher. It sounded like a cheering crowd, like when Jerry played baseball in high school, that time he screamed a line drive through the gap and scored Iggy Templeton from first. Everyone loved him for a moment, and then no one cared. This crowd cheered microscopically, tiny lungs and pin-thin bleating throats. He turned to face them. They laughed at him, squealed. They seemed just overhead. He grabbed upward.

"Most people don't try to touch them," the woman said from behind him. "Most people get creeped out first time they see them."

"What are they?"

"Bats. A goddamn million of them. A lot of people think they're birds or bugs at first."

"I can't see them." He wanted to. They sounded like a wall, a blanket of screeching. The stagnant, arid air whirred. A thousand-wing thrum. Jerry's head buzzed. He'd never wanted to witness anything so much.

"You're not bullshitting me? You really can't see them?"

"I hid my glasses under a rock."

"Well, that sounds really fucking stupid."

"Idiotic."

The bats continued to scream overhead. Daylight was a sliver to the west. There would soon be nothing to see but dark.

"And you can't see me?" the woman said.

"Legally blind since I was ten. Coke bottles, they used to say."

"You still don't get to grab tits willy-nilly."

Touch seemed so far away from him now. Sight was only a slice of fading light. Even the dry heat and the burning mesquite seemed muted. Texas reduced to a wall of bats screaming into the night sky.

"Don't move," the woman said. Jerry wondered if she had the mace out again.

The woman's footsteps crunched. He lost track of her steps. He tilted his head upward and let the screeching seep into him. For a second, he worried they might shit or piss on his face. He didn't care. Maybe he'd get rabies and be discharged. Go mad, animalistic, ravenous and wild. He'd go home and stomp on his brother's brainy bifocals and touch his brother's wife's breasts, and no one would be able to fault him. He'd be done learning about jet-fuel fires. With his disability pay, he could buy the house he grew up in, the house where his mom died of cancer and his dad had a heart attack, and he could burn that fucker to ash.

"Hold still," the woman said, behind him again. Her fingers fumbled at his temples, slid smooth plastic onto his nose. And then he could see. The bats streamed in a line, much thinner, he was sure, than that blanket of screeches he'd first heard. Off to the south, it looked like a black cloud. The bats were prowling.

"My husband's. He was blind as a bat, too." The line of bats strangled off until it was just three or four tumbling after one another. "I don't know why I still keep them in the glove compartment."

"They're good," Jerry said, and they felt right.

"They sleep under the overpass. Come out every night to eat. Come home every morning." The woman's voice was quiet over his shoulder. Every word was clear and breathy. He heard the flick of a lighter, smelled smoke. And the bats looked like that, off in the distance. Smoke from the mesquite fires. Smoke from this lady's lips.

"It's not a million of them. Only like a hundred thousand. But have you ever seen that many of anything?" She stayed close. The cigarette smoke burned bitter in his nose. He felt her body hovering like a shadow, a smoke-cloud swarm of bats. So close to touching, but something you couldn't hold. He could turn around and look and see how old she was now. He could find out what kind of woman she might be. Maybe she'd be beautiful and want to fuck, or she could spray him in the eyes and take back her glasses and leave him here until the bats returned in the morning light and he was late for another day of burning helicopters.

Jerry didn't turn to her, didn't find out. He kept watching the bats. Just a couple more lonely stragglers over him now, estranged from their group. They tripped foolishly through the electric-blue twilight. Even with the lady's glasses, they were becoming invisible. They blended into the nothing of night with perfect invisibility.

To order or obtain more information on these or other University of Nebraska Press titles, visit nebraskapress.unl.edu.

CPSIA information can be obtained at www.ICGtesting.com
Printed in the USA
LVOW11s0851230916

505936LV00001B/106/P

9 780803 288546